I0624956

Diversion

Ahab's Folly

By Jerry Bader

ISBN Paperback: 978-1-988647-73-9

Hard Cover: 978-1-988647-74-6

Ebook: 978-1-988647-75-3

The Matsumae Man

The ancient fishing boat got as close to Benten Island as possible before Kok Ji-Won is deposited in a rubber dinghy and told to row the rest of the way. It is too dangerous for the North Korean RGB agents disguised as fishermen to get any closer to the Japanese shore. They are already too close. Making it back to port in the derelict trawler is a fifty-fifty bet at best.

Kok does the best he can rowing, considering he has an attaché case handcuffed to his wrist. By the time he makes his way to the rocky shore of Benten Island near the Itsukushima Shrine, it's dark. He's soaking wet and exhausted, but this is an opportunity, not a time to go soft.

Success means a promotion, a hero's welcome, and the perks that go with being a national treasure; failure means a firing squad. The choice is not a choice. Kok sinks the dinghy as instructed with the AK47 bayonet he was given as his only means of protection. He's to meet a female agent at the *torii* gate of the Itsukushima Shrine. She's to drive him into Matsumae where he is to hand-off the documents and receive further instructions. After sinking the boat, Kok makes his way up the rocky embankment to the gate and waits.

He sits under the shrine shivering for two hours. He is sure he'll die of pneumonia before she arrives; he is wrong.

Finally, a figure appears approaching the gate. Kok can tell it's a woman by her slight build and the elegant way she moves. It looks like she is holding something in her hand, a gun. It doesn't surprise Kok, after-all, this is a clandestine operation, a gun seems appropriate, perhaps she'd give it to him. The dark figure comes closer.

"Kok, is that you?"

"Yes, I've been waiting... two hours."

The female raises the gun and fires. A nasty blood bindi erupts in the middle of Kok's forehead. He falls backward dead. She stands over him, her legs straddling his lifeless body. She puts two more bullets in his chest. She takes out her mobile phone and photographs the scene. She emails the proof of kill to her superiors.

She opens the briefcase, rips-up some of the documents, and lights several others on fire. She puts out the flames before they completely consume the pages. She leaves the briefcase open so some of the documents will get scattered by the wind. She kicks some pebbles on top of the remaining papers so they won't be blown away. When she's satisfied her mission is complete, she turns and leaves.

~

Haru Endo is a proud man, some would say arrogant. At thirty years of age, it's unusual for someone who never worked for any police department to become a CIRO Agent, but Endo had one important skill that made him invaluable to the *Naicho*, Japan's intelligence service; he was fluent in multiple languages, Korean, Mandarin, Cantonese, Russian, and English. Some of his colleagues resented the young Endo for what seemed like a meteoric rise from academic obscurity to CIRO Agent, but Endo didn't care what they thought. He knew the key to intelligence is deciphering the meaning hidden in language influenced by culture, a skill the Cabinet Intelligence and Research Office prized.

The position of CIRO Agent is an elite post if you consider the agency only has one hundred and seventy employees and reports directly to the Prime Minister. It's a plum job for an ambitious man eager to climb the bureaucratic ladder. Perhaps, someday he would be Deputy Director, or maybe even Director.

He was told to take a week off before he received his initial assignment. He decided that he would take the time to visit Matsumae Castle, an Edo period fortress on Japan's northernmost main island, Hokkaido.

Hokkaido is known for its volcanic Mount Asahi, caldera lakes, geothermal springs, and Mount Yotei, a Mount Fuji look-alike, but none of these things are what prompted Endo to make the long trek from Tokyo. Neither is the Matsumae Castle or even the rebuilt Itsukushima Shrine on Benten Island, an island in name only. It's a peninsula that juts out from the bottom of Hokkaido. This is just the kind of reference that can cause foreign intelligence to be misinterpreted. Islands aren't necessarily islands, threats aren't necessarily threats, and innocuous statements may not be innocuous at all. No, the real reason Haru Endo wanted to visit Hokkaido is what the local press calls the Ghost Ships of North Korea.

Every year dozens, some years hundreds, of dilapidated North Korean fishing boats wash-up on the shores of Hokkaido. More often than not, the boats contain the remains of North Korean fishermen. Sometimes these fishermen turn-up minus their boats. Because of the sanctions imposed on North Korea, the country is desperate for cash. Fishermen are sent out into the Sea of

Japan to steal fish from Japanese territorial waters so they can be sold to China for the hard currency the Kim regime needs to operate. The boats are often in such a bad state that they are overwhelmed by the rough seas and end-up in pieces on the rocky shores of Hokkaido.

The *Naicho* thought it prudent to investigate when one of these North Korean fishermen shows up with a bullet in his head and an attaché case filled with what appears to be documents from the Reconnaissance General Bureau, North Korea's equivalent of the Central Intelligence Agency. Since Endo was already on his way to Hokkaido and he was fluent in Korean, he was told to forget the vacation and investigate.

Where's Sidney?

Mercury and I sit eating breakfast, discussing the completed renovations that Billy oversaw at the London Bowley. As you already know from my previous reports, Mercury is my partner in both carnal and aesthetic pleasures. She runs my Toronto gallery while Billy runs the London operation. I am also in business with a friend, Sidney Katz, who runs The Smoke Shop restaurant and lounge. Since we have a rather well-to-do clientele featuring entertainers, politicians, and just plain rich people, we decided it would be clever to open the wall that separates the gallery from the restaurant. It would allow patrons to browse the gallery's offerings while waiting to be seated in the dining room. I realize most restaurants would rather have their guests wait at the bar consuming mass quantities of booze, but I figure the sale of one canvas from an upcoming abstract expressionist more than makes up for a few lost gin and tonics.

I got the idea from a place that used to be popular back in the day in Toronto. *Ginsberg and Wong* was a mashup of a joint that combined a delicatessen, Chinese food emporium and what amounted to an old fashion neighbourhood smoke shop selling all kinds of colourful and silly gadgets, junk, and candy, but no smokes. Diners browsed and even purchased some of the useless Five-and-Dime *tchotchkes* while waiting to be seated. My concept is meant to be a bit of an upgrade. As usual, I digress into the trivial, but it comes with the brief. You want comprehensive reports outlining my every action, rationale, and what-not, whether significant to national security or not, then that's exactly what you're going to get, complete with immaterial anecdotes that may not move the plot but are both informative and interesting in their colourful meaninglessness. That said, I'll move on.

Mercury and I have decided to spend more time in London, something the Circus has encouraged since my Quandary duties seem to be increasingly demanding of both time and energy. The move is made possible because Mercury, the consummate gallery professional, has trained a new director for the Toronto Bowley, a nice young man, Thomas Cohen, who has proven himself competent, honest, and a great art salesman.

I hear a faint buzzing coming from my desk located at the other end of the loft. Mercury looks up from her Eggs Benedict, "It's your phone. Mine is right here," she points to her phone sitting beside her orange juice. I take my phone out of my pocket and show her. It remains silent.

Mercury's beautiful features go hard, "Well, you better answer it. Maybe it's Harriet." More about Harriet later. I never do know who reads these reports or whether or not it's the same person each time or someone new. As such, I find it prudent to go over old ground, just in case you're new to my contemporaneous meanderings.

The phone in question is a burner provided to me by Milo McTavish a colleague, who works for the same boss as I do, Roger Ames, Head of Quandary Research. The firm is a necessary ploy due to the fact our mini band of SIS agents operates semi-legally in-country.

Technically, Quandary is a Security Service operation, but only because one of our associates, Melinda Byrnes, comes from the MI5 agency silo. Melinda and I have a bit of history that can best be described as tension release under extreme circumstances, but any further explanation or details are both unnecessary and potentially damaging to my relationship with Mercury. She is more than understanding and open-minded. She even accepts Harriet as a reality, but all women have their limits, and I dare not test them with the potentially volatile element known as Mercury Collins.

I walk across the flat, take the mobile out of my desk drawer, and answer, "Yes..."

"Hello, Quee. It's Plick."

The words hit me like a two-by-four to the gut. I look at Mercury, who has followed me to my desk. She sees the blood drain from my face. Milo is using the cryptonyms he gave us during the Mozart's Medicine operation. I have to think hard to recall all the silly names Milo gave us when using these burners. He interrupts the silence, "Your presence is required post-haste."

I needn't ask if there's a problem. He wouldn't be calling on this device using code names if there wasn't. "Where's..." I pause trying to remember Roger's cryptonym, "the Huntsman."

"Chasing Geishas from what I gather, but I'll fill you in when you get here. In the meantime, your mate needs a word."

He hands someone the phone. "Hi boss, it's me." It's Billy, my man in London.

I have to be careful in whatever I say. "Did something go wrong with the construction?"

"Not exactly, maybe..."

The phone goes silent for a few seconds, then what sounds like muffled bickering. Milo comes back on the line. "Not to worry, *old chap*, just a bit of an extermination issue. It's been resolved for the time being."

Old chap is not something Milo would normally say in conversation, that's Roger's goto upper crust turn-of-phrase, signalling me the *extermination issue* is Quandary business, not restaurant-gallery business. "Bugs! You found bugs in The Smoke Shop?"

Milo: "Aah, yes... nasty little creatures, but they've all been eliminated. We definitely wouldn't want them to migrate to the upper floors (*that's where my Quandary mates have their headquarters*), but more about that when you return. One more thing, *old chap* (*there it is again*), it seems your dinner partner has gone missing..."

He leaves the last bit hanging in the air to age like a dead duck after the hunt, then silence, for what seems like an eternity. The *dinner partner* reference is to Sidney Katz, my partner in the restaurant. Is his sudden and unplanned absence related to the bug problem?

Finally, I answer, "We're on our way."

Harry's Back In Town

I've been back only twenty-four hours, but things are starting to take form. Billy has taken charge of running The Smoke Shop, representing my interests in the restaurant. Sidney has an excellent staff and a top-notch manager, so his absence is hardly noticed. No one seems to want to discuss how Sidney's disappearance is or is not, related to the euphemistically described extermination issue. Finding surveillance bugs one floor below Quandary headquarters is not good news. Mercury, Billy, and I decide Mercury should run the day-to-day operations at the London Bowley until Sidney either returns or is found. Mercury also keeps in close contact with Thomas to make sure the Toronto operation keeps running smoothly.

Mercury and Billy decide to work together on a marketing plan for the official reopening of the integrated gallery-restaurant. I'm busy with Quandary meetings, getting caught up on why Roger is in Japan. The missing Sidney issue is another matter that needs to be resolved but is put on the back burner for the time being.

The bug problem most likely has nothing to do with Sidney's absence. His disappearance could be nothing more than an unplanned gambling

junket to Monaco. The more likely culprit is my
old pal, Yang Guozhi, newly appointed Minister of
State Security for the PRC, who likes to keep
close tabs on me and my mates.

Milo explains that Roger is in Japan investigating
the murder of a North Korean RGB Agent that
turned up with a bullet in his head and two more
in his chest. There is also the matter of an attaché
case filled with RGB documents handcuffed to
the dead man's wrist. According to the CIRO
Agent that is investigating, it looked like the as-
sassin tried to destroy the documents but was
interrupted before the job was complete. What
remains of the material describes the kidnapping
for ransom of a wealthy British citizen refer-
enced only by the name *Yolisa*. The plan is described as the first in a series of kidnappings intended to raise hard currency for the North Koreans, while at the same time inducing fear in the
wealthy capitalist boardrooms of the West. The
documents sketched out a scheme aimed to
blame well-known underworld elements in the
various target countries. In Britain, the Church
Gang, led by Carson and Carlyle Church, are the
target patsies.

The fact that Sidney is missing seems to be unre-
lated. He is rich, but not rich enough to warrant
such attention. On the other hand, he is my

friend, and the inheritance I received from my rich late Uncle might make me the real financial target. My expanding association with the Circus seems to be a link that can't be ignored. I may be the connecting tissue of the plan. Of course, these things could all be coincidences, but as Harriet is fond of saying, "... in our business, my love, there is no such thing as coincidence."

Roger left instructions for me to be in charge of Quandary until he returned. I instruct Milo to follow-up with the police regarding Sidney's disappearance while Darlene is tasked with weighing through the myriad of RGB moneymaking scams. I tell Edward and Graham to check with our Vauxhall Cross masters for any local North Korean activity. Melinda and I plan to pay the Church brothers a visit.

Milo sticks out his hand. It holds a small device that I recognize as a bug. "Perhaps you can find an opportunity to plant this in an appropriate location when you visit. I'll arrange for a team of Melinda's old colleagues to monitor the gadget if you can get it placed." I take the bug from Milo's chubby hand and slip it into my jacket pocket.

~

Tommy Lee liked to gamble, but his occupation required that he abstain from his favourite pastime. As a member of the 738 Triad, one of London's most influential and dangerous criminal enterprises, Tommy knew the consequences of not following orders, but gambling is an addiction, and addicts take risks that ultimately end with deadly consequences.

Tommy's job was simple; every evening, he would have dinner at Li Bai's Napoleon Grill, the Bonaparte Casino's dining room. Dinner was always special because the chef, a world-renown Chinese master, Li Bai, is the headman. Li made a fortune lending his name to restaurants in New York, Toronto, and London, but he especially liked working for the Church brothers because of his fondness for high stakes Texas Hold'em cash games. In London, Li could run a restaurant and gamble in one convenient location.

After dinner, Tommy would purchase ten thousand pounds worth of chips. He would play Blackjack for about twenty minutes, always making small wagers, never winning or losing very much. The object of the exercise was not to win or lose but to establish for the authorities that he was a legitimate casino patron, there to play Blackjack or as the French call it, *Vingt-et-Un*.

Of course, his real objective was quite different; Tommy Lee was a loan shark, there to launder money made from the 738's other even less respectable enterprises. Tommy's instructions were to sit at the bar and wait for Chinese gamblers down on their luck to approach him for a loan, something he was glad to do for the extraordinary fee of ten percent per week. The Bonaparte Casino was Tommy's personal franchise as authorized by the 738. If an unfortunate punter failed to pay on time and in full, it meant broken limbs and terrifying calls to the wife and children. It was Tommy's responsibility to make sure his clients always paid and for the most part, they did. The fear of 738 retribution almost always did the job.

But as I said, Tommy liked to gamble, and he was an addict. When I say was, it's because the exotic Kam Won-Sook, put a bullet in the back of Tommy's head in the alley behind the Bonaparte Casino. The same Kam Won-Sook that but a bullet in the head of Kok Ji-Won and two in his chest as he sat under the *torii* gate of the Itsukushima Shrine on Benten Island, the island that isn't an island. Tommy's mistake was taking the vig he received from a client and blow it in an all-night poker game in the basement of the Huli Jing Restaurant & Fortune Cookie Company, owned by a known MSS asset, Ho Feng, the man that runs the 738 Triad.

All of this is related to me by Melinda, while on our way to visit the Church brothers who operate the Bonaparte Casino. They technically don't own the casino but why quibble over semantics. The paper owners are upstanding men of commerce who needed the aid of the brothers to sort out certain financial difficulties. When you ask the Church boys for help, they are more than happy to oblige in return for a favour that comes in the form of an eternal obligation; namely, doing whatever the fuck they tell you to do. Despite Scotland Yard's copious files filled with reports of alleged misconduct committed by the charming but maniacal twin miscreants, no charges were ever laid. The meeting promised to be interesting. I was not disappointed.

When Melinda and I arrive at the Bonaparte, I flash my fake DCI Caul credentials to the receptionist who asks us to wait. The phoney credentials and name are an artifact given to me by Roger during the Mozart's Medicine operation so I could stick my SIS nose in business that rightly belonged to Scotland Yard or our friends in MI5. Melinda and I watch and wait. Occasionally, I wink at the security camera that seems to undress us as we sit. Finally, we are ushered into the directors' office.

Waiting for us are the brothers' Church, Carson and Carlyle, almost identical twins in every aspect of appearance and attire. Both are fifty-something pseudo gentlemen, handsome, well-groomed, and outfitted in the finest Savile Row and Turnbull & Asser bespoke tailoring. One brother sits behind a massive mahogany desk mostly clear of files or personal knick-knacks except for a very nice Remington bronze of *The Broncho Buster* and an Apple laptop. Despite the custom finery, these two see themselves as cowboys. The sitting Church sees I notice the sculpture. His eyes brighten, or perhaps, it's just his ego shining through. He smiles, "It's an original." I smile in return, acknowledging his discerning good taste.

My eyes move to the standing Church. He brushes his finger across his nose. He's positioned himself behind and to the side of his sitting sibling. His arms hang loose beside him in a somehow nonchalant yet menacing manner. Neither brother establishes which Church they belong to. I imagine the twins have used that confusion to deceive and divert since they were teenagers. But I'm distracted. Hanging beside the standing Church is a familiar painting. I get a sinking feeling and an adrenaline rush simultaneously. I turn to look at Melinda. She notices the painting as well. It is the work of Girolama Spera, real name Yang Hu, a Chinese painter who uses the infamous Italian name as her *nom de plume*. Yang is the daughter of the People's Republic of China's disgraced ex-Minister of Science and Technology and the niece of the current Minister of State Security, my old friend Yang Guozhi, but of course, all this is in the files and is well-known in our circle of Circus clowns. Hu, herself, is, or at least was, an MSS asset, murderer, and all-around pain-in-the-ass. The sitting Church turns and looks at the painting and then at me, "You an art lover, DCI Caul?"

I shrug in as casual a manner as I can muster, "I like nice things like most people."

"I can see that by your choice of partner."

I literally feel the chill that exudes from Melinda's every pore. "Perhaps it's my partner that chose me, and not the other way around." Melinda stands and sticks her Security Service credentials in front of the sitting Church's face.

He smiles a professional smile, "It looks real."

"Oh, it's fucking real alright." She uses just the right tone of hurt female pride and anger. I use the distraction to attach Milo's bug to the bottom of the chair I'm sitting in. Neither Church notices. Melinda snorts in what I assume is mock disgust. Message delivered, she sits down.

The sitting Church smiles. His brother leans over his shoulder, opens the laptop and types something. When he's finished, he returns to his menacing silent position. The sitting Church turns the computer until it faces me. It displays a news photograph of Billy and me at an opening of an exhibit at the London Bowley. Church leans forward over the top of the computer screen. His manner stays professionally polite. "You're an interesting man, DCI Caul, or do you prefer Harry Rasske?"

If you've read my previous reports you are aware that Rasske is currently my official name which differs from the one I was born with due to that unfortunate Lucy's Breath business of a few years back. "Does it matter? In either case, the visit is official."

"In that case, let's stick with DCI Caul. So then Detective, what can I do for you and your lovely partner?"

I turn and give Melinda a nod. She responds quickly, "You're playing footsie with the wrong people. They're setting you up to take the fall for some very nasty business. It's common knowledge that the Bonaparte allows the 738 to launder money on your premises but frankly that's not our concern. Our interest is more in the realm of national security. The 738 has ties with the MSS and that makes for a very sticky bowl of rice for a couple of grifters who think they have the Kung Pao shrimp by the tail."

I decide to put in my two cents, "The fact that you have a painting hanging in your office that was done by a known MSS asset isn't a coincidence. It sets you up for what's to come, And trust us, you won't like it."

The silent Church leans over his brother's shoulder and whispers something in his ear.

The sitting Church responds, "We'll be in touch."

We've been dismissed. We get up to leave. Melinda and I accomplished what needed to be done, but before I reach the door, I decide to dangle one more Columbo-style hook in the water.

"Just one more thing." I had their attention. "What do you know about the disappearance of one Sidney Katz?"

The silent Church brushes his finger across his nose. Finally, he speaks, "As my brother said. We'll get back to you."

Melinda opens the door and looks at me, "It's a miracle, Harpo, speaks."

Naicho's Man

Back at Quandary things are beginning to take shape. Roger is back, and with him is the CIRO Agent, Haru Endo, *Naicho's* man assigned to investigate the dead RGB asset. He brought translations of what was left of the documents found on the dead North Korean. The initial analysis didn't reveal much; only that the purpose of the programme, now dubbed, Ahab's Folly, is to kidnap prominent wealthy businessmen in Western Europe and the United States.

The initial target was only described as *Yolisa*, which Endo informed us is Korean for chef. I raised the idea that *Yolisa* might be Sidney; he isn't a chef, but he did run a restaurant, and as far as the North Koreans may be concerned, it was close enough. Roger thought the idea was a bit of a stretch and that Sidney probably took off for Monaco to play some baccarat and get laid. But why go to Monaco when you could take a taxi to the Bonaparte and lose your money to the Church brothers who would gladly provide a willing and attractive shoulder to cry on for a few quid more. The Church boys do pride themselves in being full-service degenerates.

Edward and Graham thought the Sidney connection had merit based on what they learned from our Vauxhall Cross masters. It seems our old enemy from the Mozart's Medicine case, Yang Bo and his artist daughter, Hu, are back in play, with revenge on their minds. Bo is the ex-Minister of Science and Technology, and his daughter was his agent involved in a money-laundering and espionage ring designed to steal high-tech military secrets. But our Quandary gang put an end to the scheme in a rather dramatic and deadly fashion.

Bo was punished for his failure and stripped of his high-profile government post, but the Yang clan runs deep in the People's intelligence community. His brother, Guozhi, Minister of State Security, holds a widely differing agenda and sometimes works with our little group for mutual benefit. But blood is blood, and it appears Guozhi has cleared the way for his sibling to reemerge as head of the People's Cyber Intelligence Committee (PCIC), a special hacker unit under the umbrella of the United Front Work Department of the Central Committee of the Communist Party. The operation is located in Shenyang, in Liaoning Province where North Korea's Bureau 121 hacker units are trained and operate under the guidance and direction of the PCIC.

The UFWD is responsible for strong-arming vulnerable diaspora Chinese in the West, people with relatives still in China. Using the cover of cultural conferences and other goodwill missions, the UFWD forces successful and influential Chinese expats to use their wealth, position, and power in service to the homeland. Part of the department's agenda is to support North Korea's efforts to divert the West's attention so the People's government can continue with its industrial, military, and political espionage efforts.

Yang Bo appears to be the man in charge of Bureau 121, the same hackers tasked with raising hard currency to pay China for keeping the Kim regime afloat. Guozhi must assume helping his brother resurface in the intelligence backwater dealing with the crazy North Koreans would keep him too busy to get involved in payback, but in our business, assumptions can be deadly.

Bo has his private programme of maleficence attached to the operation, namely revenge on his brother, Guozhi and the Quandary Research group that together put a dagger in the heart of the Ministry of Science and Technology's Mozart's Medicine industrial and military espionage operation. As Director of the PCIC, Yang Bo has an opportunity to implement his trifecta of theft, diversion, and revenge. The Yang brothers are the intelligence community's version of the singing Gallagher clan.

Darlene's research unearthed a variety of schemes the RGB tried over the years to raise the cash needed by Kim to keep his nuclear ambitions alive and his army generals stocked in Western luxuries. One of the more inventive schemes took advantage of holes in the SWIFT global bank transfer and payment network. The breach allowed North Korean hackers to divert eighty-one million US dollars belonging to the Central Bank of Bangladesh from the Federal Reserve Bank of New York to the personal accounts of several RGB assets with bank accounts in the Manila National Bank of the Philippines. Intelligence reports traced the scheme back to an infamous subgroup of Bureau 121, known as the Lazarus Group. The highly skilled hackers work out of Shenyang in China and are under the direction of Yang Bo.

Melinda and I briefed the group on our meeting with the Church boys and how they recognized me as someone other than DCI Caul. We also described how Melinda's semi-feigned feminist diversion allowed me to plant Milo's bug. Milo informed us the Security Service surveillance crew is installed in the building next door to the Bonaparte Casino and they are already receiving some interesting intelligence. The Church boys contacted their friends in the 738 to warn them MI5 and the Criminal Investigation Unit (CID) may be on to them. It didn't appear to be a concern. The 738 are used to being under surveillance. What the Churches didn't tell them was we warned them they were being set up. Perhaps they were not as confident in their relationship as they would like everyone to think. They also discussed their doubts about the new loan shark the 738 installed in the Bonaparte to replace Tommy Lee. She seemed to be an odd choice.

After some discussion, Roger decided it might be a good time to put one of our people on the floor of the casino. A gambler in need of cash would be able to establish a relationship with the new 738 loan shark while at the same time keep an eye on the Church brothers. None of our Quandary people fit the profile. What we needed was someone who would blend seamlessly into the existing predominately Asian Bonaparte clientele. Endo, our visiting Naicho agent, wasn't Chinese but he is fluent in Chinese and Korean which would allow him to pick up any loose conversation from people not expecting him to understand. The Japanese and Chinese written languages do share some symbols and grammatical forms, but verbal communication does present a challenge. As it turns out, Endo is a perfect choice.

A Girl Just Wants To Have Fun

Endo spends his evenings at the Bonaparte playing blackjack. The agency provided a twenty-five thousand-pound bankroll to establish him as a high-roller. His cover is a senior ranking Japanese government official in London to close a deal with The Advance Cyber Group: an Israeli company specializing in developing security software for government agencies. The rumour is TACG is financed by a secret venture capital fund of the Mossad whose products do a lot more than provide security protection. The Israeli government is tight-lipped about their involvement, but our Vauxhall Cross masters' arrangement with the Israelis is telling.

The cost of Mossad's cooperation is the inclusion of a Kidon agent, a secret unit of the Metsada, the Mossad subgroup that specializes in assassinations and sabotage. The Kidon agent assigned would only identify him or herself if necessary, in which case, the agent would use the code word, *Fedallah:* the secret harpooner Ahab brings onboard to kill Moby Dick.

If Yang Bo is the psychologically maimed, obsessed captain, and Quandary is the giant white whale, then that makes me, Ishmael, the narrator of this still unwritten tale.

As instructed, Endo loses several thousand pounds a night, after which he takes his frustration out on a bottle of Yamazaki Single Malt Whisky, hoping to attract the attention of the 738 loan shark. All the pieces appear to be in place for the white whale to finally end the captain's cursed hunt by dragging him and his ship of hackers down to the bottom of the intelligence sea. I can only hope, that like Ishmael I survive the voyage.

Mercury wants me to show her around town, so we decide to take the night and have some fun. I suggest dinner and a few games of chance at the Bonaparte, a timely and convenient distraction. I check with Roger just in case he thinks my appearance at the casino might blow Endo's cover, but he thinks the opposite. He figures my presence will divert attention away from Endo and whomever the Israeli agent happens to be.

Roger rubs his chin in a now-familiar decision-making gesture, "You think we should send Melinda and one of the boys? They'll assume we have a full team of agents working the casino, but they'll be focusing on the wrong people."

"Sure, that makes sense. It's a bit of a gamble, but they must realize we're going to have eyes all over them. Perhaps they'll see it as an advantage, figuring the presence of known intelligence assets will ward off whatever the 738 is planning. I'm sure they took our warning seriously, so they just might view our presence as welcome protection from their unreliable partners."

"Agreed. I'll make the arrangement."

Dinner at Li Bai's Napoleon Grill, Bonaparte's four-star restaurant, is almost worth the expense. More importantly, Mercury enjoys it, and she appears to be having a good time. As we share a double order of Hot Apple Beignet, Mercury gives me a strange smile.

"What? You don't like the dessert?"

"Dessert is delicious, dinner is excellent, and my companion is attentive, but what I really want to know is why we are here in a known underworld hangout, while you are an owner of your own very fine establishment?"

I open my mouth to reply, but she stops me. "Just tell me this, are we here on your other business?"

"In part, think of it as my way of multi-tasking."

"Tell me how I can help?"

"All you have to do is gamble." I slide an envelope containing five hundred quid across the table. "Anything but blackjack." She looks at me with a quirky conspiratorial smile, "Anything but black-jack..." she repeats, assuring me she understands. "Are you expecting your presence to incite some dramatic behaviour at the blackjack table?"

"I doubt it, these guys are way too smart to start anything, so let's just enjoy the evening. They'll know I'm here. That's the only objective other than providing a little excitement to your life."

She laughs, "I can't wait. I know the kind of ex-citement you get into. I was in Washington, the last time you played with your Chinese pals."

"Technically, it wasn't the last time, but why quibble over details."

"Just don't get us both killed, please."

"I'll do my best."

I watch as Mercury makes herself at home at a baccarat table. I scan the room, looking for any-thing that seems out of place. Melinda is at the roulette table while Milo quietly plays the slots. Both have eyes on Endo, who appears to be on a winning streak at one of the blackjack tables. He looks like he's been drinking pretty hard. His behaviour has become increasingly animated. I hope it's an act, and he hasn't got carried away with his covert assignment. It's not uncommon for undercover agents to start living their pretend lives for real.

Sitting at the table next to Endo's is a familiar face; it's Harriet, or someone my brain wants to think is Harriet, most likely, merely the result of some disrupted synapse in my pareidolia infected noggin. I still haven't resolved the issue of her existence. Her appearance, real or imagined, is telling; things are about to happen. Why I'm I not surprised? What part is she playing in our off-West End drama this time? More to the point, who is she working for? Is she the Israeli agent? Is that who she's always been working for, the Mossad, or is she a Langley interloper? Or maybe she's one of our own Vauxhall Cross ringmasters, here to keep an eye on the three-ring circus that appears to be playing out on the Bonaparte casino floor.

I stand at the bar beside an attractive Korean woman who also appears to be more interested in viewing the casino action than in participating herself. I notice one of the Church twins approach the baccarat pit boss in charge of Mercury's table. He whispers into his ear. The pit boss says something to the dealer, who acknowledges his understanding with a nod.

The other Church brother hovers around the blackjack tables where Endo's stack of chips is growing ever-higher along with his alcohol-fuelled excitement. I move away from the bar and find a slot machine that provides me with a view of the entire casino. Perhaps it's my overactive imagination, but I can feel the tension in the room rising. I hear a yelp coming from Mercury's baccarat table. It's Mercury. Her stack of chips has just doubled with an all-in gamble. I look over at Endo's table and see that his stack has started to dwindle along with his mood. I feel someone put their hand on my shoulder, I turn, it's the other Church.

"Your lady-friend seems to be enjoying herself."

"With a little help from your brother."

"Just our way of making you feel welcome."

We both look up at the sound of loud, rapid-fire Japanese exploding from Endo's table. I don't speak Japanese, but it doesn't take much of an

imagination to figure out Endo's outburst direct-
ed at the dealer is not a compliment. Church ex-
cuses himself and heads to the blackjack table to
try and calm the situation. By the time both
Church brothers reach the table, Endo has run
out of Japanese expletives. He heads to the bar
where the beautiful Korean woman seems to be
stationed. He takes the seat beside her. She
touches his hand, and with her other, raises two
fingers, signalling the bartender to deliver a couple of Yamazaki mood enhancers. If she is an in-
house escort, she wouldn't be buying anyone
drinks. She must be the 738 money-lender and
likely, Yang Bo's North Korean proxy.

The Chef

The following morning the team meets at our headquarters above The Smoke Shop. Melinda reports that one of the Church brothers acknowledged her presence at the casino with a comped bar bill and a smile. We still don't know which brother is Carson and which is Carlyle, but eventually, close observation will reveal some detail that will allow us to tell them apart.

Milo's evening was uneventful, but he did take note of the Korean woman cozying-up to Endo, who confirmed the woman is the 738 loan shark. He professed his antics were mostly an act, but he does admit the alcohol did help him pull off the charade. Roger warned him not to get carried away with play-acting his part.

Endo says the loan shark calls herself Camille, but Graham knew from the audio surveillance that the Churches referred to her as Kam. Milo managed to take a photograph of the woman that he sent to Darlene to check out. Darlene sent the image downtown to see if the Korean was on file.

According to the Naicho, Kam Won-Sook is a known North Korean agent who was recently spotted in Matsumae. It seems she was the contact for the RGB agents that made it across the Sea of Japan. She left Japan immediately after the murdered Ghost Ship agent was found on Benten Island, the island that isn't an island. The coincidence did not go unnoticed.

Endo's big losses and drunken antics attracted the Korean's attention. She bought him a drink, and they talked. As previously planned, he told Kam he was desperate; the money he lost was government funds intended to pay off an Israeli security software sales agent. The ruse was intended to prove to the loan shark that Endo is corruptible. The plan worked.

Kam said she would set-up a meeting for Endo with her boss, who might be willing to replace his substantial losses along with a bonus if he would do them a small favour. She said she would call him with the time and place.

Roger focuses our attention on what's next. "I've been in touch with The Institute (Mossad), and they want Endo to offer them TACG's Gorgon software. Sanctions restrict China and North Korea from purchasing the hacking spyware legitimately. The Kidon operative will act as the corrupt TACG sales agent. Endo already established the sales agent expects a payoff, so the scheme should be convincing if Endo can pull it off."

"I'm assuming the software version they're offering contains a concealed worm that will mess with their intelligence networks?"

Roger confirms the objective. "The Israelis have been working with the Five Eyes looking for an opportunity like this for some time. It just happens our operation is a perfect fit."

"What's the going price for this kind of thing?"

Roger flips through some notes he has in front of him. He finds what he wants. "TACG sells it to approved countries for $650,000 US per device, plus an additional $500,000 for installation. The Israelis want Endo to ask for 2,500,000 pounds. Anything less, and the plan wouldn't smell right."

Milo: "Sweet deal, we screw the bad guys, and the Mossad makes a profit. It's a win-win for everybody."

My phone starts to vibrate. I take a look. It's a call from Carson Church."

"Hello..."

"Harry, it's Carson Church. We need to see you immediately."

"What seems to be the problem?"

"Our chef has been kidnapped."

"I'm on my way." I hang up. "That was Carson Church. It seems the North Korean's kidnap target wasn't Sidney at all, but, Li Bai, the chef at the Napoleon Grill."

Roger: "Take Melinda."

Harry and Melinda Go To Church

When we get to the Bonaparte, both brothers are waiting for us. Melinda and I are welcomed rather enthusiastically, a far different greeting than we received the last time.

I keep my eyes open, looking for any tell that will help distinguish the identical twins. Like the last time, both brothers are wearing custom charcoal grey bespoke Grieves and Hawke pinstripe suits, custom white cotton shirts, and matching vertically striped red and black Turnbull and Asser ties. What I didn't notice the last time is one of the Churches has a habit of brushing his nose with his left hand before he speaks. Perhaps a mannerism earned from eliminating the residue of various recreational substances.

We are ushered into the same office we were in on our first visit. The brothers take their usual positions, with one brother seated behind his large mahogany desk, while the other brother takes his spot behind his sibling and off to the side. The standing brother points to the two chairs opposite and offers us a drink. He's the nose brusher.

The sitting brother speaks, "I'm the one that called you." That makes him Carson, and the standing brother, Carlyle.

"Your chef is missing?"

Carson opens his desk drawer, takes out an envelope, and hands it to me. Melinda takes a thin latex glove out of her purse along with a plastic evidence bag. Carson Church smiles and redirects the envelope to Melinda, "I see you always come prepared."

She answers in a flat, cop-like manner, "You can count on it." She opens the envelope, takes out the piece of paper, and holds it up for me to read. The letters have been cut out of the headlines in the London Times and pasted on copy paper:

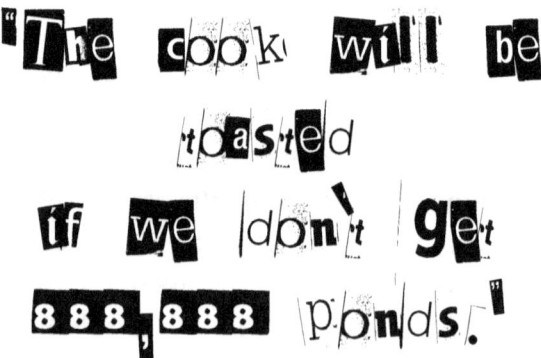

Carson looks at me with a quirky half-smile, "Not very subtle or articulate, is it?"

I half nod, "Either they want us to know it's from a Chinese speaking kidnapper, or they aren't very good at their jobs. I warned you the 738 are setting you up for something."

Carlyle brushes his hand across his nose, "These guys are smart. The spelling mistake and lucky number are too obvious. I think they're on purpose, a diversion. They must know you have us under surveillance, and we would protect ourselves by telling you. They want you to think it's the Chinese."

Melinda: "So if it's not the Chinese, who is it? Is it a rival gang or a casino competitor that wants to dump you in the deep end?"

Carson: "It's the Koreans."

Melinda and I try to look surprised but without success. Carson smiles, "But you know that already, don't you?"

"Why would the 738 put a North Korean agent in your casino if they weren't working with the RGB? They assumed you'd go to the cops who always jump to the first, simplest answer. You fellows have a reputation, so the Koreans figured the cops would take for granted that you kidnapped the chef."

Carlyle brushes his hand across his nose. It's becoming an irritating quirk, "Why the hell would we kidnap our own chef? Or, for that matter, why would the 738 point the evidence at us. It's stupid."

I shrug, "Probably to create a diversion, a misdirection to confuse and complicate something simple and decidedly more profitable. In the end, it all boils down to money, but then, who knows the mind of a criminal?"

Carson laughs, "I like you, Harry. You're a government knob, but I like you anyway."

Melinda seems a bit frustrated, "Jesus Christ, can we move on, or do you two need a moment?"

I shoot Melinda a look. We need to build a rapport with these guys if we want their co-operation, but I move on, "They'll be in touch with a time and place for the payoff. I assume you'll co-operate?"

Carson: "Cost of doing business, Li Bai is quite the draw. People come to eat because he's world-famous and they stay to gamble. We'll pay."

"Let me know how and when they want to get paid. If it's cash, we'll need the serial numbers so we can trace the money. If it's digital, we'll handle the transfer."

Carlyle rubs his nose, "Forget it. We're not giving you access to our accounts."

"Put the funds in a new account to be used only for this transaction. After it's done, you can cancel it. We need control so we can trace it."

Carson: "That could work."

"One more thing, send us all the video of Kam Won-Sook's interaction with anyone in the casino. They might have another agent in place that you don't know about, or they could be pressuring prominent Chinese locals for favours. And that won't be good for your business."

Carson nods in agreement.

The Handler

While we wait to hear from the Churches about the arrangements for the payoff, Endo contacts Kam to tell her the sales agent is not happy about the additional request. Endo informs Kam, the Israeli demands to meet the new buyer before any sale is made.

Kam is furious and threatens Endo, but Endo holds firm. Kam offers to meet with the seller, but Endo tells her the Israeli already warned him not to fuck-around. It's the Israeli's ass on the line if TACG finds out about the illegal sale. If the sales agent doesn't meet with the principal, the whole deal is off, including the legal sale to the Japanese government. Kam finally relents, telling Endo she'll inform her handler. An hour later, Kam confirms the meeting.

Kam, her handler, and Endo are to meet the following day at two o'clock in the afternoon in the lobby of the Langham London. When they arrive, Endo will get a phone call with further instructions. Roger makes arrangements with the Israelis. The meeting will take place in one of the hotel's luxury Infinity Suites giving us enough room to set up surveillance in one of the bedrooms. Milo and Darlene will handle the technical stuff while Melinda and I monitor to make sure nothing goes wrong. Edward, Graham, and Roger will be in the lobby capturing images of the handler on the chance he gets spooked or shows up with uninvited reinforcements.

The Kidon agent will only arrive in the suite after our Quandary people are in place. He or she will be wearing a disguise. To further protect the identity of their agent, the Israelis instruct us to arrange the room so their agent sits behind two powerful thousand Watt Fresnel lights aimed at the three chairs designated for Endo, Kam, and the handler.

By twelve noon, all the Quandary team are in place. We wait. At precisely five minutes to two, the door to the suite opens and a woman walks in. I take one look at her and my heart almost explodes. What the fuck is going on? Melinda looks at me and touches my hand, "Harry are you okay? You're as white as a sheet."

I shake my head, unable to speak. Am I having another of my episodes? My pareidolia infected brain has conjured up the image of my sometimes chimeric partner, but this time with a blonde wig, dark glasses, and floppy fedora. But no elaborate disguise can conceal the identity of the woman I think I'm seeing on the monitor. It's

Harriet. Or have I finally lost the plot completely? Was Harriet real and not just an imaginary side-kick dredged from the recesses of some long-forgotten B-rated Film Noir movie? Had the pressure of recent events finally made me snap? I thought I saw her at the Bonaparte, but I dismissed it as guilt for ignoring Mercury. Was I back in that place where reality and fantasy become conjoined in an elaborate intoxicating cocktail of mental confusion? Was I finally proving to myself and those around me that I was nuts? I'm sick... and lost.

Melinda stares at me with concern as sweat drips from every hidden crevice of my being. "Jesus Christ, Harry... pull yourself together."

There's a crackle in my headset; it's the rustling of the Kidon agent's clothes as she settles into a black leather Le Corbusier club chair behind the two powerful Fresnels. She flicks the switch beside her on the chair. Half the room explodes in the glare of blinding light. The woman is almost completely obscured, Endo, Kam, and the handler will see nothing but a vague outline of a woman bathed in darkness. She takes an earpiece out of her purse and places it in her ear, allowing us to communicate without our guests hearing. She takes a Beretta Pico .380 semiautomatic handgun out of her purse and places it on the arm of the chair. She rests her right hand on the gun. "Hello my love, I've missed you desperately."

"Jesus Christ, Harriet, is that really you? You're *Fedallah?*"

"Of course it's me, my love, who did you think they'd send?"

"You're real: not just some phantom remnant of an apophenia delusion?"

"Of course I'm real, silly, but deep down, you've always known. Haven't you."

"You work for the Israelis?"

"I told you, Harry, I work for the good guys. Always the good guys."

I don't know what to say. I glance around the room at Melinda, Milo, and Darlene. They're looking at me like I just stepped out of a Bethlem Royal psych ward. The door to the suite opens, and Endo, Kam, and the handler enter.

Melinda: "Holy Shit, it's the chef, Li Bai."

Harriet points to the chairs in front of her. Endo and Kam take the two end seats, and Li Bai takes the centre.

Kam: "This is bullshit. Turn the lights off so we can see who we're talking to, or I'll do it for you."

Harriet: "You move your skinny Korean ass off that chair before I tell you to, and I'll put a fucking hole in an appropriate body part."

Kam gets out of the chair and makes a move toward Harriet, but Li Bai grabs her arm stopping her. Harriet shoots anyway. Bang! "*Gae-sae-kki!* You shot me! Bitch!"

Harriet: "Stop whining. It's only a nick. And if you don't fucking sit down and shut up, I'll finish the job." Li Bai pulls Kam back into her seat.

Harriet: "Your playmate is bleeding all over the furniture, so we better make this quick. The deal with the Japanese is not your concern. As for you two, I wouldn't sell the North Koreans a bowl of used rice." Kam starts to make another move towards Harriet, but Li Bai stops her again.

Li: "I completely understand your position, but you wouldn't be selling anything to the Koreans; you'll be selling it to the Chinese. We do a lot of business with the Israelis. I believe the number is upwards of fifteen billion."

Harriet: "Sure, chef, but this ain't no crate of Jaffa oranges. And based on your pretty North Korean girlfriend, one would think our product might just end up in the hands of that crazy fat fuck with the goofy hairdo."

Li: "Perhaps a premium might help smooth the way for a resolution to your political dilemma."

Harriet: "I don't think your little fake kidnap operation can raise the kind of cash we're talking about."

Li smiles, "You seem to know a lot about our business. That could be very dangerous for someone with loose lips."

Harriet: "Don't worry about my lips, darling. I ain't no *yenta*, but the price of sale and silence is three-and-a-half million pounds."

Li: "That's a pretty big premium. A lot more than Endo told us."

Harriet: "You're not Endo. If your little kidnap operation can't raise the scratch, then perhaps you should stick to our oranges."

Li: "We can handle the price. We have another... business opportunity that can fulfill the demand. It will just take a little longer to put together."

Harriet: "You better put on your go-fast cooking shoes, chef, because my friend Endo could be called back to Japan at any time, and without him, there's no deal. So heat-up your wok and get that stir-fry in the works. When you've got the dough, call Endo, and I'll make the arrangements with him. This meeting is adjourned, my friends. Now get out before your girlfriend gets any more blood on the carpet. I really should tack on a cleaning charge to your bill, now fuck-off before I think better of this whole deal."

Li: "I'll need your name."

Harriet: "Names aren't important, my dear."

Li: "Best we have a name to reference, so we all know who we're talking to, or about."

Harriet: "You can call me, *Fedallah.*"

The Big Fortune Cookie

The 738, is run by Ho Feng, aka *Sibpal*, aka Mr. Eighteen, aka The Big Fortune Cookie. He is the PCIC agent in London. He runs the UFWD protection and influence pressure operation in Great Britain. Sibpal, his preferred moniker, is smart but without much in the way of a moral compass unless the compass in question is somehow stuck pointing to 'political zealot.'

Although Kam Won-Sook, nominally works for Sibpal, her only real loyalty is to the fat man with the strange haircut in Pyongyang; this creates a potential conflict of interest as Li Bai is responsible to the Big Fortune Cookie, who is responsible to Yang Bo, who, in turn, is responsible to the grinning Panda in Beijing, a man who barely tolerates his marriage of convenience with his capricious Pyongyang counterpart.

Sibpal runs his operations out of his offices above the Huli Jing Restaurant and Fortune Cookie Company located in the heart of Chinatown around the corner from the Da Ma Casino. It's only a two-minute walk from the Quing Dynasty gate that denotes the entrance to London's Chinatown. Although the 738 does not have a direct paper interest in the Da Ma Casino, they are nevertheless the defacto owners and thus have a direct conflict with the Bonaparte and the Church brothers. The Churches know the score and tolerate the 738 loan shark in their casino as it is the price they pay for maintaining a truce because, in the end, peace is more profitable than war.

The kidnapping of the Church brothers' world-class chef upsets the tenuous peace. The abduction and ransom demand is seen as a first strike, signalling what is to come. The Churches are unaware of Li Bai's extracurricular affiliations and, as such, see the kidnapping only as a direct assault on their business; an initial move designed to ultimately take control of the Bonaparte. They cannot let the attack go unanswered.

From the Chinese perspective, the kidnapping is a diversion, a scheme designed to focus attention on an irrelevant criminal move by the 738, while Yang Bo's daughter, Yang Hu, the artist and MSS agent known as Girolama Spera runs the main money-making scam: the hack of SWIFT bank transfers. We still don't know who, how, and from where Yang Hu plans to steal, but we do know that's their plan. Roger will inform our masters who intern will decide if the Five Eyes should be told. Informing the Canadians, Aussies, and Kiwis, is generally safe, but the Americans are another consideration. They tend to favour self-interest over communal benefit, especially the current administration. If informed, they just might decide to make a deal with the Chinese behind our backs. It wouldn't be the first time the Yanks left their Five Eye brothers hung-out to dry. It's most certainly a tricky business.

If you're privy to my previous reports, you'll know the background of Yang Hu and why she was invited to leave Great Britain with a "don't let the door hit you in the ass on the way out" sign attached. Her current presence in the land of afternoon tea was discovered by my Quandary colleague, Darlene when she routinely checked the border crossings into Northern Ireland from the Republic. The name Giulia Tofana jumped out like a lonely Granny Smith in a bin of Red Delicious. When she checked the video taken at the border, sure enough, Giulia Tofana, was in fact, Yang Hu. One would think using the mother's name of the original Girolama Spera would set-off red flags, but when you're a creative mind who thinks you are always the smartest one in any room, you do stupid shit like that.

All of this explanation is a preamble to what is about to happen next, the payoff for the phoney kidnapping plot. The entrance of Yang Hu into the mix is the rabbit hole of intrigue that pointed

Milo in the right direction so he could piece together the puzzle that is the true intent of the North Koreans and their Chinese mentors.

We debated whether or not we should inform the Church brothers of Li Bai's involvement. In the end, we decided it's best to let the kidnap payoff play-out as if we were fooled by the diversion.

We'll let the Churches pay the ransom while we keep an eye on Li. Milo and Darlene will dive into the Yang Hu angle to determine just how she intends to pull off the heist.

An idea crosses my mind, which at first I dismiss as stupid and dangerous, but the more I think about it the more it might make sense. I raise the issue with Roger.

"Roger, I had a thought, but it's probably a terrible idea. I hesitate to even raise the issue."

"Let's have it, dear boy, best we pursue all angles in this tangled web of chicanery."

"Yang Guozhi, Bo's brother... I've always had a good relationship with him. Even though he's the Minister of State Security, he hates Bo and they've always been working at cross purposes. Guozhi wants good relations with the West because he sees that as the best way to maximize the economic impact, but Bo is old school, still trying to dominate through disruption. If Guozhi knows we're on to Bo, perhaps he can put an end to the whole scheme."

"Dangerous play, dear boy... Guozhi is the one that gave Bo his job as head of the PCIC. After the Mozart Medicine fiasco, Bo is lucky they didn't line him and his daughter up against a wall. If the shit hits the fan again, it might just get all over Guozhi. The boys downtown won't like to lose an important ally, like Guozhi."

"You're right. It's a stupid idea."

"I'm not so sure. Let me run it by our Vauxhall Cross masters. They'll probably want to get the Minister involved. Let's put it on the table and let the politicians make the decision. In the meantime, carry on with what you're doing."

Arrangements Are Made

Mercury and I sit watching reruns of *Peaky Blinders* on the large screen television. My mind wanders to the George Condo on the wall and the part it played in the Mozart's Medicine business. I constantly have to keep my head free from falling into its old habit of fabricating reality out of random bits of mental flotsam and jetsam. My self-doubt is somewhat assuaged by the recent revelation that Harriet, the lovely Harriet, is in-fact a real person, and not just some misguided cerebral delusion. My mental withdrawal is interrupted by the soft touch of Mercury's hand on mine, "Come back to earth, my love. Your secret code ring is buzzing."

My mobile is vibrating frantically, demanding my attention. It's Roger, "Word has come down, old chap, Guozhi, is a no-go. Too dangerous for all concerned, including Guozhi. We just don't know if this operation is Bo's alone, part of a bigger MSS operation, or from higher up the food chain. The fat man in Pyongyang needs money, and Beijing is sick and tired of paying their way. Guozhi is most likely caught in the middle, going along to get along. There are just too many unknowns for the political cost accountants to balance the diplomatic ledger."

"Well, that's that."

"Not quite, dear boy, the powers that be think we should read-in the Church brothers."

"We read them in; there will be consequences, messy, bloody consequences."

"Nevertheless, that's what the ringmasters want. Having the gangster twins do our dirty work will distance the political heat. Besides, putting the brothers' Church in our pocket for encouraging them to remove a competitive obstacle will give us some potential leverage in the future when our involvement might be legally unwise."

"Okay, Roger, I'll set it up, but realize, drastic efforts to kill the disease can result in unintended consequences... like killing the patient."

"True, but we, lowly grunts, live in a short-term world. Long-term thinking is for academics with the luxury of time and hindsight. Our political masters in Westminster just want results. You need to tell the Churches, Kam and Li are working for Sibpal to disrupt their casino business. No need to get into the political angle."

"You know what they'll do. It will get very messy. You'll have a lot of tap-dancing to do with Scotland Yard and MI5 to clean this up and protect our new gangster mates."

"Gangster mates? Didn't quite think of them that way, but you're right." Roger pauses to think of the ramifications of what's to come. "So be it, old boy, I'll make sure everyone toes the line. National security and all that good stuff are on the line, so the bureaucratic empire builders will just have to suck it up and play along."

"Okay, Roger, I'll call first thing tomorrow."

"Take Melinda. I think the Church boys like a pretty face."

"I don't think the feeling is mutual."

~

Li Bai sits across the dinner table from Sibpal in Sibpal's private dining room in the back of the Huli Jing Restaurant and Fortune Cookie Company. Li Bai has been Sibpal's guest since his fake abduction. They await instructions from Beijing.

A messenger from the embassy arrives and is immediately ushered into the elaborately decorated private dining room. The courier stands at the entrance holding two envelopes, one in each hand. Sibpal waves for him to approach. The messenger approaches, bows, and extends his hand with one of the envelopes. Sibpal takes the envelope. He looks down at the familiar hand-written Chinese scrawl of Yang Bo on the front of the envelope, "*For Ho Feng's Eyes Only*." Sibpal looks up at the messenger, "And the other?" as he points to the envelope in the messenger's other hand.

The messenger points to Li Bai, "For him." Sibpal frowns but nods acceptance. The messenger hands Li Bai the second envelope. The message on Li Bai's envelope is similar to Sibpal's, "*For Li Bai's Eyes Only*." Li Bai also recognizes the carefully handwritten calligraphic markings, but on this envelope, the letters were formed by Yang Guozhi. Both men open their envelopes and read.

Sibpal's note is brief and to the point "*Eliminate the Churches. - YB*"

Li Bai reads his note, "*Remove Kam Won-Sook. Permanently. - YG*"

Neither man needs to be told what to do with their note. Sibpal takes a bowl of half-eaten rice that sits on the table and dumps the remaining contents on the plate in front of him. Li Bai does the same thing. Both men place their notes back in their envelopes and drop them in the empty bowls. Sibpal takes a gold lighter out of his pocket and lights the envelope on fire.

Li Ba looks at Sibpal and extends his hand across the table, Nice lighter..." Sibpal hands him the lighter. Li Bai lights his envelope on fire. Both men sit and watch the flames turn their instructions into ashes. Li Bai hands Sibpal back his lighter. Both men finish their dinners in silence.

Later that day, one of Sibpal's men arrives at the Bonaparte Casino. He asks for Kam Won-Sook. The casino host points to the attractive Korean woman sitting at the bar nursing a glass of Yamazaki Single Malt Whisky. The courier delivers the note to Kam. She finishes her drink and heads for the ladies' restroom. She checks to see that all the stalls are empty. She enters the last cubicle and closes the door. Kam reads her note, *"Take-out the Churches - Sibpal."* She drops the note in the toilet and flushes, making sure the contents have disappeared into London's ancient sewage system.

Kam already received a directive from the big man himself in Pyongyang, instructing her to eliminate Ho Feng and Li Bai once the operation is complete. That would make her the only one left in London able to run joint Chinese-Korean operations. Operating the Da Ma and Bonaparte Casinos would allow her to skim enough off the top to provide a well-earned retirement pension. While Kam ponders her good fortune in the restroom of the Bonaparte, Harry and Melinda arrive for their meeting with Carson and Carlyle Church.

The Synod

Carson sits behind his oversized mahogany desk while his brother, Carlyle, takes his usual position at his twin's side. I wonder if there is a significance to the ritual positioning of the brothers. Is Carson the real leader of the pair, due perhaps, to his earlier expulsion from their mother's crowded womb? In life, timing is everything. Or, is it the preferred arrangement, based on an agreed-upon order of merit? Maybe Carlyle likes the backseat where he can observe and advise, or maybe he just prefers to stay out of the line of fire. Whatever the reason for their now-familiar positioning, no overt sibling rivalry appears to be evident, at least on the surface. Carlyle looks at me as he brushes his hand across his nose, "I hope you and your friends enjoyed yourselves the other night?"

Melinda stays quiet. I answer. "Yes, very much. We appreciate the hospitality."

Carson leans back in his leather chair, "So what can we do for Queen and country today?"

"It's not what you can do for us, but what we can do for you."

Carlyle remains silent, letting his brother take the lead. "Really. I'm intrigued, albeit, a bit surprised at the generosity. So, Harry, my new art dealer, SIS pal, what favour are the security services of the land wanting to do for a couple of bad boys like us."

"I'm sure you remember our original meeting and our warning concerning your friends and rivals, the 738."

"Yes, we are aware. We know the 738 are the ones behind Li Bai's kidnapping. We thought it was the Koreans, and that Kam Won-Sook bitch, but it's Sibpal, he wants control of our casino."

"Not exactly. The control of the Bonaparte is merely a byproduct of the plan. And Kam Won-Sook is up to her pretty Korean neck in this deal. Li Bai wasn't kidnapped. He works for the 738, who's doing the Korean's dirty work. The Chinese are sick and tired of paying the freight and taking the heat for Pyongyang's craziness. They want the Koreans to start paying their way. The plan is a way to raise money for the North Koreans. This is just the first of a whole series of kidnappings. The operation just fell into Sibpal's lap, a lucky coincidence. He can make his Chinese bosses back home happy and fuck you in the bargain."

"So, this Kam broad being dropped into our casino is no coincidence. She's not just working as a loan shark for the 738, she's North Korean intelligence."

"That determination is yours. We didn't say that, but you can come to your own conclusion."

Carlyle rubs his nose, "So in return, I gather you want us to back off? Because if that's the deal, the answer is no."

"You're free to handle the situation whatever way you see fit. You'll get no interference or blowback from the security services."

"And the police?"

"We'll clear the decks of any annoying police repercussions. As long as there's no collateral damage, they'll be no undue consequences."

"Assuming we can trust you government knobs to keep your word, nothing comes without a price. A favour given is a favour earned. So, what do you want in return?"

"We'll get back to you on that... someday, some time, somewhere."

The Heist

By the time Yang Hu, now calling herself Giulia Tofana, arrived in Great Britain, her crew of Bureau 121, Lazarus hackers were already in place in the basement of the Huli Ji Restaurant & Fortune Cookie Company. Like Hu they arrived in the country from the Republic, making their way across the border into Northern Ireland, then on to London. They crossed the border with phoney South Korean passports as part of a tourist group sponsored by a South Korean travel agency known to be a RGB/MSS front.

Hu is feeling the pressure from her father, Yang Bo, to finalize the purchase of the Gorgon software and get out of the country before she's discovered. This time around, she is operating without diplomatic cover. Failure would not bode well for her or her father. The thought of a potassium cyanide capsule is a decidedly unappetizing end to her spotty secret agent career.

The SWIFT bank heist was originally designed to pay for the Koreans infiltration into the London casino business; now, it's needed to pay for the Gorgon spy software as well. The appearance of Endo as a corrupt Japanese official seemed to prove to Beijing and Pyongyang that the strategy of infiltrating the London underworld was a stroke of genius.

As much as the public would like to think that the international banking system is secure, history tells us a vastly different story. The belief that once burned, institutions would be forced to institute higher levels of protective spending is more wishful thinking than reality. And so, the Lazarus hackers believe, since the SWIFT heist of the Central Bank of Bangladesh worked once, it will probably work again. It is hard to think the North Koreans would have the balls to try it a second time, but nerve is something Pyongyang has in abundance. This time the target is the Central Bank of Madagascar's deposits in the Bank of England.

The success of the 2016 operation depended on audacity, brilliance, and good luck. The theft wasn't perfect, but it did garner a hundred million US dollars for Pyongyang out of the targeted one billion. Perhaps the sheer magnitude of the attempt raised red flags, but if it wasn't for a sloppy misspelling of the word, *Foundation,* in the name of the recipient NGO, the whole jackpot might have been pocketed. This time the hackers need to be smarter. For the Yangs and their hacker minions, failure is not an option.

The plan is to transfer ten million pounds from the account of the Central Bank of Madagascar in the Bank of England to the account of the KWS Import-Export Company in the Industrial Bank of Macao. KWS is solely owned by Kam Won-Sook whose instructions are to withdraw the funds immediately upon receipt. Three million pounds are to be used to purchase the Gorgon software, while the seven million remainder is to be laundered through the Da Ma Casino. Eventually, the excess funds will finance the takeover of the Bonaparte Casino. Once the Chinese and their pals in the Korean intelligence service control two major London casinos, they will be able to self-finance their combined espionage operations. Controlling the high-profile gambling operations will create potential financial pressure that can be used to influence politicians and industrialists who suffer from a fondness for games of chance.

The specifics of the attack are not relevant for those of us on the ground and should be left to the cyber boffins in Vauxhall Cross to dismantle and decode. What we do know is the hackers are fond of using malware that has many names, the most popular being Dridex, but it has also been called Bugat and Cridex. The malware captures banking credentials used to redirect bank transfers using a process called injection attack. These attacks are made possible by a backdoor to the macros used in Microsoft Word. Any Windows user who opens an attachment in Word or Excel is open to this kind of malware. I include this basic information in my report for context, so the reader understands the nature of these kinds of crimes. I am sure our group of ex-HM Belmarsh alumni working off their extended prison terms can provide more details to the nitty-gritty of the matter. For Quandary, the when, where, and who are the points of interest. The how is left with those whose brains are more mathematical than my rather abstract asymmetrical manner of problem-solving.

We assume the heist will be taking place soon since the funds are needed to purchase the Gorgon Software. Roger has informed our friends in the Five Eyes so they can each keep an eye on any unusual glitches occurring in their central banks. The Prime Ministers of Bangladesh and Madagascar have also received calls from our PM so they can inform their intelligence agencies. The entire effort is a bit like trying to find your keys in a locksmith's workshop; the effort is more symbolic than functional, but now, no one can accuse us of keeping vital information to ourselves. Protecting our political asses is always a major concern in these matters.

The Payoffs

While we were putting together the pieces, Hu and her hacker pals were busy robbing the Central Bank of Madagascar. As one clever wag at head office correctly but sarcastically pointed out, *we were rather a penny short and a day late*. With the cash in hand, Kam calls Endo to set up a meeting to purchase the Gorgon Software. While this was happening, the Churches receive a package delivered to the Bonaparte that contains a Hello Kitty backpack and instructions on how to deliver the ransom for Li Bai.

The Churches were kind enough to inform us of the payoff, although they did decline to accept our help or tell us the details. Their reluctance to have us tag along wasn't a problem since we acquired all the details from the bug I previously planted in Carson's office.

As it turned out, both payoffs are about to happen simultaneously. That meant splitting our limited Quandary forces. Most of the crew is charged with monitoring the ransom payoff as it seems to be the scenario that had the greatest likelihood of blowing up in everyone's face. Milo and I are assigned to the software sale. The arrangement suited me just fine, as I am not overly fond of situations that might explode in heavy gunfire, and it did mean another opportunity to see Harriet, albeit remotely.

The software sale is to take place in the John Snow Pub, located on Carnaby Street, famous for its mod fashion revolution in the swinging sixties. Carnaby Street is a pedestrian shopping area in Soho. During its heyday, the street boasted the legendary Marquee Club, the favourite hangout of bands like The Who and The Rolling Stones. In those days, the area featured trendy fashion designers like Mary Quant. On a sunny Sunday, you might bump into Twiggy or, maybe Brigid Bardot, window shopping for some new offbeat threads.

The John Snow Pub pays tribute to the famous physician who discovered the cause of the 1854 cholera epidemic caused by a tainted water pump on Broad Street. His findings led to the locking of the pump, resulting in a rapid decline in cholera cases. The name is a bit bizarre for a food and drink establishment, but it does speak to Harriet's rather quirky sense of humour, tainted water, the metaphor for corrupted software.

Kam is to bring the cash to the John Snow at the same time the Li Bai ransom is being paid. Harriet and Endo will arrive after Kam enters the pub. The money is to be delivered in one of those travel suitcases on wheels, the ones with an extendable handle. Prior to the exchange, the pub will be swept by head office techs. Vauxhall Cross will also provide a couple of people to aid in the surveillance, one to act as a bartender and the other a busboy. Milo and I are restricted to the kitchen, as our appearance would put a violent kibosh on the whole deal.

As things are getting complicated, a review of the facts we know, and the facts we don't, might be in order. We know Yang Bo is in-charge of the joint Chinese-North Korean operation to infiltrate shady London casinos. Control of the casinos provides entree into the London underworld so as to gain influence over local Chinese industrialists and political leaders who have gambling problems. Influencing competitive states through pressuring expatriates is China's primary political operational objective.

The secondary goal is to help the North Koreans raise significant sums of money to pay for China's help in keeping the Kim regime afloat. To raise these funds, the Koreans replicate their 2016 SWIFT bank heist of Bangladesh deposits on account at the Fed, but this time, the target is Madagascar's cash-on-hand in the Bank of England. The whole kidnapping scheme is a diversion intended to distract the various British intel-

ligence services, so they focus on the kidnappings while the North Koreans rob vulnerable
central banks.

The fly in the ointment is Yang Bo and his ill feel-
ings toward me, my Quandary mates, and his
brother, Yang Guozhi, the Minister of State Security, who has a profoundly different view of
what's best for his country. There are details we
are not aware of at this time. These hidden elements speak more to the personal agendas of the
people involved than they do to the overarching
geopolitical goals of their masters. In a word or
three, these objectives are best described as
cleanup, revenge, and greed.

When the payoffs go down, we are unaware Sibpal told Kam to kill the Church brothers so he
could take control of the Bonaparte without the
nuisance RGB getting in his way. What Sibpal
wasn't aware of was Yang Bo instructed Li Bai to
eliminate Kam Won-Sook as he too had little use
for the North Koreans. What none of them real-
ized at the time was, the seemingly ultra-loyal
Kim partisan, Kam, had ideas of her own.

The instructions for the Li Bai ransom payoff are
clear and specific: place 888,888 pounds in the
Hello Kitty backpack provided. Carson and Carlyle, together, are to take the backpack to Soho

Square Gardens and leave it at the base of the back of the Charles II statue in front of the octagonal, gazebo-like "Tudorbethan" cottage located in the centre of the park. The payoff is arranged for Saturday noon when the park is at its busiest. It will be extra busy this Saturday due to a charity concert by a local klezmer band. The Churches are instructed to go to the concert and wait. Once the money has been retrieved and counted, Li Bai will be released. The scheme is simple enough, except for the planned aftermath. Kam Won-Sook has been ordered to kill the Church brothers during the concert. But the Churches have a plan of their own. The brothers have instructed their minions to lunch at the Huli Ji where they are to order bullet-riddled Sibpal on a platter.

The octagonal hipped-roof of the quaint "Tudorbethan" cottage is supported by timber columns that provide a gazebo-like setting for visitors that want to keep out of the sun. The historic cottage has a second-story under the dramatically pitched roof. The eight-sided second-floor room has windows on all eight sides, providing a 360-degree view of the park from where Kam intends to use her high-powered sniper rifle to eliminate the Church brothers during the concert.

Once the mission is complete, Kam will breakdown the Chinese sniper rifle and stow it in its custom guitar carrying case. The park will be busy with concert-goers; no one will pay any attention to Kam as she leaves the cottage with her deadly, hidden instrument.

The Churches have a plan of their own. Perhaps it lacks the sophistication of the Sibpal operation, but it never-the-less seems to be effective. The Churches have a busboy who's been working in the Huli Ji kitchen for months, waiting for the chance to be useful. He was put in place to pick up any interesting 738 chatter. Since he is already in place, he becomes the perfect person to smuggle weapons into the restaurant, enabling the Church assassins to arrive unarmed.

The busboy uses a large, deep, metal tray to clear tables. He'll place the weapons in the tray to hide them. When he cleans the assassins' table, he'll deliver the guns. The rest is loud and messy, but hopefully for the Churches, effective. We know all the details of the plan because of my bug. Permanently eliminating the 738 leader from the playing pitch may not be legal or ethical, but it does serve a greater purpose. Best of all, our hands are clean, well, not exactly clean, perhaps just soiled around the edges. Of course, we all know what happens to the best-laid plans.

Shite Happens, Part I
The Concert

As Kam looks out the window at the frenetic musical performance of the Kenton Klezmer Band, she realizes just how privileged she has been. She's never heard this kind of music before, or seen such an odd assortment of characters that make up the band. The group consists of three men and two women. The men wear black suits, white shirts and colourful ties. Each man wears a different style hat. The floor bassist wears a black Fedora, the washboard player wears a black Campaigner, and the handheld keyboard player wears a Porkpie. The two women are dressed in long dark dresses with multicoloured shawls wrapped around their shoulders; one plays the violin and the other a clarinet.

All are middle-aged but move around the stage like raptured Sufi Dervishes. The crowd responds with sheer delight and enthusiastic participation. Kam has seen things and done things her fellow North Koreans would never have imagined existed, but this is something new, and she likes it.

Kam always thought of herself as a sophisticated woman, having travelled the world in service to her Supreme Leader. She's led a privileged, but extraordinarily unorthodox life. As a child, she was taken from her subsistence existence and placed in a school where for twenty years, she was educated, indoctrinated, and trained to be a killer that could blend into Western society while fulfilling her mandate of disruption.

She understood her life was both a blessing and a curse. A blessing, because she could partake in the freedoms and benefits of the West. An advantage denied to almost every other North Korean citizen, even those that were considered the elite.

A curse, because she knew she could never go back. Going back meant certain death. There was no room in the Supreme Leader's tightly controlled society for an outlier. Despite her excellent record and fierce loyalty, she knew she would be considered a corrosive influence, corrupting those with whom she came in contact.

When her usefulness to the man with a strange haircut ran out, she knew what awaited her. She could never go home; she needed a plan, and this operation provided the means to avoid her inevitable fate. Her eyes move from the stage to the Charles II statue. There is a crowd around the statue, but everyone is transfixed by the band and their music. She spots the Church brothers approach the long-dead king. Carson is carrying the Hello Kitty backpack. She smiles; the colour-ful child's bag conflicts with Carson's usual sarto-rial sophistication.

Her Zijiang M99 semi-automatic sniper rifle leans against the wall beside the partly open window that provides a clear view of Charles II and the Churches. She picks up the rifle.

She follows Carson through the scope of the rifle as he places the bag at the foot of the statue as instructed. The brothers move off into the crowd. Each goes in a different direction. She doesn't want to lose them, but she must make sure the money is picked up by the courier. She spots a kid on a bicycle hurrying through the crowded grounds, zig-zagging to avoid hitting any citizens. He speeds by the statue and in one swift ducking motion grabs the bag and races off.

With the money safely secured, she searches the crowd for the Churches one more time. She spots Carson eating an ice cream cone. She aims and squeezes the trigger just as an elderly woman steps in front of Carson. She's hit.

Kam swears,"*jojdwaess-eo!*" She fires again, but Carson dives for cover. She frantically looks for Carlyle. When she spots him, she sees he's aiming a Beretta semi-automatic in her direction. He fires, shattering the glass window in front of her. Kam drops the rifle and heads for the stairs. She feels a wet gooey substance drip down into her eye. She's been cut by flying glass.

She races down the stairs and out the door. The band continues its frenetic performance. Most of the crowd hardly notices the botched assassination. A group of concerned citizens gather around the wounded old lady. Kam loses herself in the chaos. She's fucked!

Shite Happens, Part II
Dim Sum

Four men in business suits enter the Huli Ji and order Dim Sum. The men talk business, the stock market, and golf, just like you'd expect from any group of Paternoster Square professionals. The men order *Char Siu Bao*, *Char Sir So*, *Cheung Fun*, Chicken Feet, and *Dan Tats* for dessert. The food is accompanied by healthy quantities of rice wine. Satisfied with their meals, the men sit silently while the Chinese busboy clears the table and delivers four Heckler & Koch MP5K machine pistols, one for each man.

The men get up from the table and make their way to the kitchen. The hostess in her red and gold cheongsam spots them and calls out, "Private! Staff Only!" The men disregard her and enter the kitchen. They are ignored by the busy imported Hong Kong staff. The hostess rushes in after them, calling for them to stop. She sees they are carrying machine pistols. She screeches, "STOP!" One of the men turns and fires over her head. She dives for cover, stumbling over her long dress. The Chinese staff all race for the fire exit.

The men continue through the kitchen and enter a hallway with two guards standing in front of double doors. They go for their guns, but too late. The assassins fire multiple rapid rounds. The guards go down. The intruders kick open the double doors and enter the fortune cookie factory. About a dozen elderly Chinese men and women turn and look at the four Caucasians carrying deadly submachine guns. They stare for what seems an eternity but is only a second, then go back to work. Standing on the mezzanine balcony that overhangs the factory floor is Ho Feng, aka Sibpal, Mr. Eighteen.

Church's men let loose a barge of continuous fire, shattering windows, light fixtures, and the glass wall that separates Sibpal's office from the mezzanine balcony. Sibpal dives for cover through the shattered glass. Two of the assassins rush to the metal stairs that lead up to the office while the other two turn to see three of Sibpal's guards try to enter, but their way is blocked by the elderly workers trying to leave. The intruders hesitate, not wanting to hit the old-people. One of Sibpal's men fires, hitting one of the assassins in the shoulder. But, he is still able to return fire along with his partner. The guards go down in a heap. The intruders make their way up the metal stairs to join their associates. They rush through the fire exit to the outside landing joining their colleagues as they watch Sibpal race away in his Mercedes GT Coupe.

The Software Sale
The Gorgon Spreads Its Tentacles

Perhaps the most important aspect of the Ahab's Folly operation is getting the corrupted Gorgon software into the hands of the Chinese and North Koreans. The application will allow our side to combat the digital mayhem our Asian counterparts are so fond of creating. Unlike the Li Bai kidnaping payoff and the Church assassination attempt on Sibpal, the software sale should be relatively free of chaos.

If you are wondering, what happened to my colleagues who were supposed to make sure what happened at the Soho Square Gardens concert and Huli Ji Restaurant, didn't? The answer is simple. The bright brains safely tucked away in their Vauxhall Cross offices decided to allow my colleagues to observe only. And so, Roger, Edward, and Melinda stood around watching Kam Won-Sook and the Church brothers screw-up their planned mutual annihilation while Graham and Darlene sat quietly consuming Steamed Crystal Dumplings as mayhem ensued around them at the Huli Ji.

I am sure these memos that I file go through a rigorous redaction process. There is always the chance an inquisitive *Guardian* journalist might file an FOI request on the goings-on at the Soho Gardens concert and Huli Ji Restaurant & Fortune Cookie Company. My suggestion is the person responsible should use an extra-thick Sharpie for the job. But then I am just an art dealer masquerading as a secret agent, so my sarcastic suggestions will most likely be chalked-up to extreme bitterness, which may be well-founded. Moving on ...

The sale of the Gorgon software is arranged to take place at a sushi bar in Covent Gardens. The busy high-traffic location is chosen in an effort to eliminate any violent attempts at coerced negotiations. However, the notion of hiding behind the public's metaphorical skirt didn't seem to work in either the Soho Gardens or Huli Ji scenarios.

Participants in the software sale's meeting are Haro Endo, our Naicho colleague, pretending to be a corporate, gambling-addicted, Japanese government purchasing agent; Harriet, my sometimes silent partner and Kidon Agent, pretending to be a greedy TACG salesperson; and Kam Won-Sook, fresh from her botched assassination attempt on the Churches, and currently scrambling to avoid the consequences of one of the Supreme Leaders deadly hissy fits.

Milo and I position ourselves at a table protected by an oversized potted geranium tree but still with a clear view of the entire restaurant. We hope everything goes down without a hitch, as the city and the agency have seen enough collateral damage to last everyone a very long time.

Harriet and Endo wait at a table for four. Kam Won-Sook arrives, wheeling a black suitcase that contains either three million pounds or her get-the-hell-out-of-town-quick-kit. Kam stops at the door scanning the room for danger. She spots Endo and Harriet but doesn't see us. Endo waves to attract her. She's annoyed at the extra attention. She is uncharacteristically nervous, which under the circumstances, is not surprising.

Kam approaches Harriet's table and sits. Five minutes earlier, Endo placed a miniature directional microphone on the underside edge of a plate overflowing with Makizushi so Milo and I can hear everything that's being said. Kam looks around the room but still doesn't see us behind the giant geranium.

Kam: "You brought the software?"

Harriet: "Two thumb drives as requested. You brought the funds?"

Kam: "In the suitcase."

Harriet: "Mind if I check?"

Kam slips a small laptop from the outside pocket of the suitcase, "First, the thumb drives."

Harriet unfolds the linen napkin beside her plate of Sashimi, revealing two small thumb drives and a Beretta 92FS 9mm semi-automatic. The man sitting at the table next to them sees the gun. He whispers something to his female lunch date.

Harriet notices. She looks at the woman, smiles, then at the man. Harriet places her index finger to her lips, signalling the couple to mind their own business. She pushes the thumb drives across the table but doesn't remove her hand. Endo flips over his napkin, exposing a matching Beretta. He places his hand on the pistol. Kam attempts a smile, but it turns into more of a smirk, "Well, aren't you the well-equipped pur-chasing agent."

Endo: "*Okane o kudasai*...the money."

Kam looks at Harriet, then back at Endo, "Aah, very nice. I see you have become partners."

Endo: "The money!"

Kam pushes the suitcase towards Endo. "Take a look. It's unlocked." Endo flips open the latches; he looks inside. "It's all there. Why fuck around?" Endo snaps the suitcase shut. He nods to Harriet, who removes her hand from the thumb drives. Kam slips the first thumb drive into the laptop's USB port.

Milo taps me on the arm. He points out the window. A black Porsche Cayenne pulls up and parks illegally in front of the restaurant. A heavyset Chinese man gets out of the driver's seat. He comes around to the curbside to open the backdoor. The wind catches his unbuttoned black suit jacket revealing a semi-automatic strapped into a black leather shoulder holster. He opens the back door of the SUV. Li Bai gets out, followed by Yang Hu, previously known as the artist Girolama Spera, and currently operating under the alias of Giulia Tofana. They enter the restaurant, look around and approach Kam's table.

Li Bai takes a position on one side of the table while the heavyset driver stands opposite. Yang Hu takes the empty seat beside Kam. I notice Kam flinch ever-so-slightly, probably from a pistol being poked into her side. Hu takes the thumb drives from Kam.

I start to get up, but Milo stops me. He points to the door of the kitchen. My old friend Yang Guozhi, Minister of State Security, and three rather athletic-looking Chinese bodyguards exit the kitchen. They go straight to Harriet's table. Two of Guozhi's bodyguards approach the table first. One takes Hu's driver by the arm while the other grabs Li Bai and escorts both out of the restaurant. They are unceremoniously pushed into the illegally parked Porsche and told in Chinese to "*GUNDAN!*" No translation is needed.

Guozhi politely acknowledges the couple at the table next to Harriet's. He says something to his remaining bodyguard, who takes one of the extra chairs at the table and places it beside Harriet. Guozhi picks up the leather folder that holds the bill for the couple's meal. "Please, may I pay for your meal? It is the least I can do to make up for the interruption." The man nods and mumbles a thank you. He grabs his dinner companion and hustles out of the restaurant.

Guozhi looks at Hu, "Hello, Niece."

Hu: "Hello, Uncle."

The bodyguard goes to where Hu is sitting. He sticks out his hand. Hu looks at her Uncle, "Fuck!" She hands the bodyguard the two thumb drives.

Guozhi takes Kam's laptop from her and checks to see if his niece hasn't made a switch. She hasn't. Guozhi sticks the two thumb drives into his pocket. He hands his bodyguard the laptop.

Hu looks at her Uncle. "What about the money?"

Guozhi: "A sale involves an exchange of valuables, in this case, money for software. I have the software. They have the cash. Seems fair. Best you move along."

Hu: "What am I supposed to tell my father?"

Guozhi: "I think the Americans have an expression, 'if at first, you don't succeed, drop back ten and punt'."

Hu: "What the hell is that supposed to mean?"

Guozhi: "I have no idea, dear Niece, but I suggest you leave the country as soon as possible. Otherwise, your old pal Harry Rasske and his friends might find you. You never know what geranium plant they may be hiding behind." The son-of-a-bitch knew I was there the whole time.

Hu looks at Kam, who sat nervously through this whole exchange: "And what about her?"

Guozhi: "Not my business. That's between my brother and his friends in Pyongyang. I think it's time for you to leave." She hesitates for a second, says something under her breath, then gets up. Guozhi's bodyguard escorts her out of the restaurant to a waiting limousine.

Guozhi turns to Kam. "I believe running is your best option, or perhaps asylum somewhere as far from your Supreme Leader's reach as possible. You might even be able to retrieve that seven million pounds you still have stashed in Macao, but perhaps not. I believe it is time for you to skedaddle. Funny word, skedaddle, English is such a very silly language." Guozhi makes a motion with his hand, signally Kan Won-Sook to disappear. She gets up and heads for the door, looking over her shoulder several times.

Guozhi turns to Harriet, "Always a pleasure, my dear Harriet, always a pleasure. I'm sure we will meet again. And please say hello to my old friend Harry. I believe you can find him behind an ancient geranium tree in the corner of the restaurant." He turns to Haro, "Mr. Endo, so nice to meet you. Please give my regards to my *Naicho* friends. They do try so very hard." Yang Guozhi gets up and leaves with the two corrupted Gorgon software installers.

A Grand Old Party

Being busy with my recent Quandary duties has placed my personal life on the back-burner. During my absence, Mercury and Billy worked hard on the relaunch of the Bowley-Smoke Shop Restaurant and Art Gallery Complex. It appears my absence was hardly noticed.

Tonight is the grand opening, and I have to admit, I am eager. The place looks great. Mercury and Billy have done a tremendous job. The invited dignitaries from the press, art, and political communities have started to arrive. Staff are gliding around the complex like gold medal ice dancers. The paintings, atmosphere, and environment result in a surge of red dots on almost every work-of-art. It is going to be a very profitable evening.

My duties are to stand by the door and greet visitors as they arrive. Mercury reminded me to be amiable, no matter how hard it was for me to stomach. I find smiling for more than a few minutes to be a strain, but I've learned to take Mercury's suggestions like orders from on high.

As invitation-only guests file-in, I shake hands, smile, and point to the maitre d' who invites them to peruse the artwork before taking their assigned seats. There, they find a small hand-signed, limited-edition lithograph by the featured artist of the evening. It was an expensive bit of swag, but as promised, it appeared to be producing a sold-out opening.

The artist, a quirky raconteur with a mop of dreadlocked orange and purple hair, entertains the guests with humorous tales of the people he's met and the life he's lived. A lifestyle, from what I gather, has seen its fair share of chemically-fuelled debauchery. I'm not sure how much of it is true, but it is most certainly entertaining, and more importantly, effective in producing a multitude of red dots.

An invitation was sent, at my request, to my old frenemy, Yang Guozhi, without any anticipation of him accepting. London is a long way from Beijing in more ways than mere distance. It was my silent postscript to the Ahab's Folly business.

To my surprise, he walks through the door with an attractive female embassy aid and two large bodyguards. The sight of Yang and his uninvited non-RSVP protection prompts Mercury and Billy to go into a frantic recalculation of seating arrangements.

Guozhi approaches me like a long-lost friend. He puts his arm around my shoulder in an almost fatherly manner and guides me off to a quiet corner. His date and plus-two hover nearby.

The sight of the PRC Minister of State Security creates a ripple of buzz that radiates through the restaurant and connected galleries like a wave at a Blue Jays' playoff game.

His voice is low but firm, "I have news…" He pauses as he looks over his shoulder, spotting one of the large abstracts hanging on the wall. "I do like that one. Shame, it's already sold."

"I can arrange a commission. I am sure the artist would be pleased to add you to his colourful anecdotal repertoire."

"Yes, that might be fun, we shall talk, but in the meantime, as I have said, I do have news." I remain silent, waiting.

He smiles. "Kam Won-Sook has been sighted in Macao playing baccarat at the Parisian. It seems she decided to keep the seven million pounds that found its way into a Macao bank. The Supreme Leader is not happy and has ordered her head delivered on a platter. Personally, I don't give a damn, but he's decided that my brother and niece are to blame, which may be true, but still…" He pauses one more time before continuing, "We may have our differences, but they are family, and what can I say? We all have relatives." He looks at me for confirmation. I don't reply.

He continues. "In any case, old friend, if you decide that an ex-RGB agent might be a welcome addition to your lovely island, and if that sanctuary happened to be disguised as a revenge assassination, I would be most appreciative. Removing her from the field of play might help take the heat off my brother and niece.

"Your superiors might not feel the same way."

"My superiors have a rather complicated relationship with the mercurial Supreme Leader. He is more than a bit of a pain-in-the-ass. He serves a purpose but needs to be kept in line. Your intervention would serve everyone's purpose, and besides, our mutual goodwill has always been positive in the past. so why spoil a good thing."

"I don't know, Guozhi, she's a bit of a wild card. My bosses might prefer her dead for real."

"That would work, but don't be naive, Harry. She's an asset. She might not provide the keys to the kingdom, but she would be a significant public relations coup. One that might produce a green ink memo of thanks for your service."

I like Guozhi, but he is a tricky bastard that often plays both sides of the ball at the same time. Getting us to give Kam asylum might be a setup, a plant, aimed at placing her in our system to garner useful intelligence. Maybe they discovered the Gorgon software had a virus, and this was payback. And, if we expunge her from the living, they just might expose our complicity. This little scheme of Guozhi's was way above my pay-grade.

"Does Roger know Kam's whereabouts?"

"I leave that to you, Harry, but it might be better to fly solo on this one. Besides, I've heard rumours that your friend is also in Macao, and he seems to have run into some serious trouble."

"My friend?"

"Sidney Katz, your missing partner, I'm sure you haven't forgotten about him." In fact, I have.

Guozhi signals his female friend, "I think I will see if I can find that artist of yours. Maybe he's interested in a commission for my office." He starts to walk away but turns to add one final postscript. "Congratulations on what seems to be

a very successful opening. Be well, my friend."
Guozhi moves off with his entourage in search of
the artist.

Three Days later...

The Hotel Parisian Macao is a strange place, but
oh so very twenty-first-century China. It is both
dripping in extravagant faux European luxury,
while at the same time, bizarrely kitschy. The
complex features a half-size Eiffel Tower and imi-
tation Renaissance lobby with ceiling frescos
worthy of the most outrageous Las Vegas tourist
trap. It is depressing to think that four hundred
years of combined Portuguese and Chinese art
and culture has produced this, but then China is a
nation that does have an entire city dedicated to
mass-producing cheap knockoff masterpieces to
match the couches of the creatively illiterate.

When Guozhi told me Kam Won-Sook has been
spotted playing baccarat in the Parisian casino, I
hesitated to act, but when he mentioned Sidney
was in trouble, I had no choice but to move forward. I cornered Roger at the opening. He was
sitting at a table with my Quandary mates. I told
him what Guozhi said. He also hesitated. The
next day we met, and arrangements were made. I
was on the next plane to Macao.

As far as we know, we accomplished embedding the Gorgon software in the Ministry of State's computer. The intelligence had already begun to filter in. The job now was to determine if any of it was useful, or even real. In our business, real is an elusive ideal.

The second and perhaps most important objective of infiltrating the RGB system appeared to be stalled. It seems Guozhi wasn't inclined to offer his brother and his pal the Supreme Leader access to the Gorgon application. The Big Panda appeared to be onside with Guozhi. He obviously decided that the software was more useful as a bargaining chip when dealing with his unpredictable neighbour.

My arrival in Macao is without incident, except for the fact I think I see Harriet getting into a cab at the airport. As you are aware from my previous reports, Harriet tends to appear when things get sticky. What I previously thought was merely my overactive imagination, has turned out to be real, and not a fantasy. But still, seeing Harriet always gives me pause and a not so gentle shot of testosterone. I now know she is real, but my sightings of her are sometimes more wishful thinking than proof of life.

Unintended Consequences

Some weeks earlier...

Sidney sits in the darkened restaurant staring into space. The Smoke Shop is due to reopen in the next few weeks. The renovations are almost complete. All that remains is the return of Harry and Mercury to London and the opening gala. The gallery space that connects the restaurant to the Bowley is blocked by a four-by-eight foot poster of an abstract portrait done by the colourful painter to be featured at the relaunch. But Sidney doesn't see any of it. He doesn't hear the rain hitting the front windows, nor does he hear the tapping of his foot on the newly installed black slate floor. All he hears are the voices on the SD card he removed from one of the devices the Church brothers demanded he attach to the new light fixtures that hang over every table in the restaurant.

What he expected to hear was the sounds of the Italian construction workers arguing with the interior designer over how to do each other's job, but amongst the miscellaneous chattered were the sounds of familiar voices, the voices of Harry's colleagues who occupied the offices on the second floor above the restaurant. Sidney knew, or at least thought, Harry was involved in something, but this was too much. The installation of the devices was forced upon Sidney because of the gambling debts he accumulated at the Bonaparte. The Church brothers gave him a choice, pay in cash, body parts, or install the recording devices in the lights above each dining table.

The restaurant's clientele of industrialists, politicians, and celebrities made for a plentiful source of useful gossip. The Churches could use this material to put pressure on the diners that also frequented the Bonaparte in futile attempts to win back the substantial sums lost at their tables and were either unwilling or unable to pay. As far as Carson and Carlyle Church were concerned, the work-product from the devices was mere leverage, a practical means of obtaining what was rightfully theirs, but Sidney knew better. This scheme was blackmail, pure and simple.

Sidney could live with his participation in the plan as long as all his limbs remained attached and his debts were paid-off. But this latest development shone a whole new light on the situation. Sidney knew Harry had secrets. He'd always seen him as a Jay Gatsby-type: rich, intelligent, and connected to something most likely nefarious. He never expected he was SIS, and he never considered the possibility of Harry's friends being MI6. But there it was, loud and clear. Amongst the bickering workmen's palaver were intelligence briefings and discussions of government operations from the people he'd grown to know, people he'd served regularly in the restaurant: the pedantic Roger Ames, the pretty lawyer, Melinda Byrnes, the affable clown, Milo Mc-Tavish, and the others, Darlene, Edward, and Graham, all intelligence agents.

What he was doing was espionage. Whether the Churches were aware of this or not didn't matter. Unintended consequences could be as deadly as owing a hundred thousand quid to a couple of well-dressed gangsters. He'd have to remove all the devices before the sun came up and before the workmen arrived to complete the final finishing touches. He'd destroy everything, including the SD card audio produced. He was sure Harry's pals knew about the devices. They wouldn't be very good at their jobs if they didn't. Once he removed the evidence, he'd run. He'd clear out his bank accounts and disappear somewhere far from the Churches and far from the reach of Harry and his government friends.

Murder In Macao

I arrive at the hotel to find a flurry of police activity. It seems they're there to investigate the misadventure of some poor soul whose splattered remains decorate the roof of the massive steel and glass portico that fronts the architectural ode to overindulgence known as the Hotel Parisian Macao. I've learned, in such circumstances, it is best to mind one's own business and proceed as if this was a normal daily event, probably one Tripadvisor is unlikely to promote. I have issues of my own to deal with, a seemingly rogue RGB agent and a missing partner. I doubt Kam has gone over-the-bamboo-wall, despite my pal, Yang Guozhi's, advice. It all smelled too much like an elaborate MSS-RGB plot to infiltrate the halls of Vauxhall Cross.

I have no time for sore-losers who decide taking a walk out the twenty-fifth-floor window of their over-priced hotel suite is the best way to settle a series of bad beats at the poker table. The act of defenestration has become all too frequent in my life, as you may be aware from my previous reports. One hopes it doesn't foreshadow my own ultimate earthly exit. Mercury would surely shed a tear or two. The problems at hand are certainly more pressing, as nothing more could be done for the late hotel guest whose body parts now littered the hotel entrance's roof.

After checking-in, I decide to take a nap. I don't want the jet lag to dull my idiosyncratic approach to problem-solving or trigger any more fanciful visions of the lovely Harriet. When I wake, I shower and dress to go down to the main dining room for dinner, but before I do, I decide to check out the casino.

If I thought the casino would be any less of a *nouveau riche* extravaganza than the rest of the place, I thought wrong. The casino assaults the senses like the aftermath of a kill room in a scene from *Dexter*. The walls, carpet, and gaming tables are thick with blood-red paint, wool, and felt with the occasional splash of gold to add a Louis IV flavour to the now more entrepreneurial Little Red Book adherents' money trap.

Red is a favourite colour of the Chinese as it symbolizes luck, joy, and happiness, not a bad trifecta for an over-the-top gambling joint, but any interior decorator I ever met will tell you the overuse of deep passion red can cause the heart to race and the hackles to rise, probably not the best thing for a casino full of losers.

Out of the corner of my eye, I spot a woman. She quickly turns away, avoiding my attempt at recognition. Is it Harriet or merely a mental mirage signalling danger ahead? The woman disappears into a crowd of gamblers celebrating a winning hand. I scan the room in an attempt to track her down, but my Harriet is as elusive as her frequent imagined apparitions.

She's gone. I must admit the likelihood of her never being there in the first place is very real. The thing is, I now know Harriet is real, even if all her on-screen appearances are not. I scan the room, again searching more pragmatically for Sidney and the deadly Kam Won-Sook. I fail to find either.

I feel a tap on my shoulder. I turn. It's a Church. The well-dressed gangster twin runs his finger across his nose in what has become his distinguishing gesture. "Well, well, if it isn't the brother Church, known as Carlyle."

He smiles at my ability to distinguish *Thing One* from *Thing Two*. "Harry... it's the nose thing, isn't it?" He's not really asking, just ruminating on the potential of a habit that could cause him trouble. He continues, "What are you doing here?"

"Gambling."

Gambling? I thought gambling was a no-no for you spy-types?"

"Ever hear of James Bond?"

Carlyle laughs, "Sure Harry, I've heard of Bond, but you're no 007"

He's right, of course, but I'm still annoyed at his slight. I decide to move the conversation off of me and onto him. "And, pray-tell, what are you doing here?"

"Checking out the competition."

"Hardly competition, when it's 9600 KM away from London."

"Not for gamblers, Harry, not for gamblers. Besides, you never know who you're going to run into when you visit the competition. People run-up debts in one place, but instead of paying what they owe, they merely move on to another more receptive establishment. The distance can be seen as an advantage."

"So you are the collection arm of the Bonaparte Church?"

"As I said, Harry, I'm here checking out the competition."

"Check them all you want; just don't get in my way. Or we might decide to make things difficult for you back home."

He runs his finger across his nose. "Ditto, old boy. ditto." It's not quite a threat, more of a challenge. He smiles, then runs his finger across his nose one last time for good luck and moves off.

I am a bit surprised at the talkativeness of the brother Carlyle. My experience to date has revealed that Carson is the chatty Church, while his brother is the taciturn mirror image. As you already know from my previous filings, I have a fondness for the rotund Kasper Gutman's turn-of-phrase. Like Kasper, *I am a man who likes talking to a man who likes to talk.*" Talking can reveal hidden secrets if you listen carefully, but it helps if you know to whom you're talking.

Have the evil prankster twins decided to run a game on old Harry? Was the nose thing a charade of misdirection, a diversion, a purposeful canard to make me think Carson is Carlyle? Is the gambit for *Thing One* to distract me, while *Thing Two* does the dirty work? The brothers' Church are a shifty pair, together they combine to form a

Yin and Yang of unsettling maneuvers. I must think on it for a bit.

Perhaps a medium-well-done-steak and a couple of Vodka Collins' will help the mental digestion of the facts. The Parisian Macao dining room is slightly less ostentatious than the casino, but not by much. The designers must have finally got the message across that too much red in the eating area might put the losers off their feed. Let the suckers relax and linger over a few too many whiskies, making them more amenable to blowing the rest of their wad on the tables. Aah... free enterprise, Chinese style; not so very different from the capitalist version.

Now that I am fed and rested, I decide it is time to do my job. My first stop is the concierge to see if I can find out if any of the bad actors in this Chinese opera are currently on the Parisian stage. The Assistant Manager is a pretty young woman with a bright smile. Her cheery disposition quickly sours when I ask, "Can you please tell me what room my friend Sidney Katz is staying in?" Her only response is a blank stare.

I try again, "I'm supposed to meet my friend Sidney Katz for a drink, perhaps you could try his room? He appears to have over-slept."

The young woman's face turns from a blank stare into a slow-motion animation of empathy and sadness, climaxing in fear. Tears start to well up in her eyes. Suddenly she turns and runs into the back office. Women may not generally fall to their knees at the sight of me, but then, neither do they start to cry and run and hide. I must admit to being slightly nonplussed.

I hear a bit of a commotion coming from the back office, mostly Cantonese jibber-jabber mixed with hysteria. Finally, a middle-aged gentleman comes out wearing a funeral director's expression and a name tag that identifies him as Mr. Hong, Hotel Manager.

He speaks perfect English, "You were asking about Mr. Katz?"

"Yes. We were supposed to meet for a drink, and he didn't show up. I assume he must have been tired and over-slept."

"I'm afraid..." he pauses for a brief moment to find the words, "I'm afraid Mr. Katz is no longer with us."

"When did he check-out?"

"He hasn't checked out. The thing is, he owes a substantial sum for his room and other amenities. I'm afraid his credit card has been declined. Perhaps as a friend, you would like to clear up the amount outstanding."

"What do you mean he is no longer with us?"

"Mr. Katz is dead."

"Dead?"

"There was an accident."

"An accident? What kind of accident?"

"You're Mr. Raaske aren't you? You checked in earlier today I believe?"

"Yes, that's correct."

"You saw the commotion out front when you arrived?"

"That was Sidney?"

"I'm afraid you'll have to speak to the authorities if you want any further information."

The Manager's expression remains blank. He
picks up some nonessential papers that happen
to be in front of him. He scrutinizes the documents as if they were from Mao himself. I've been
dismissed. I must admit, I am stunned. I quickly
come to my senses when a rather large officious
man in a rumpled grey suit thrusts what I assume is a Macao police detective's ID in my face.
He is accompanied by a younger plainclothes po-
liceman who stands several paces behind.

"Raaske, Harry, the art dealer?"

"Aah… actually, it's the other way around…"

"Excuse me?"

"Never mind, officer… ?" He flashes his badge one
more time. "… Sub-commissioner Li. What can I
do for you?"

"You were a friend of Mr. Katz." It's a statement,
not a question.

"Yes, we were business partners in London." That
was a mistake. Never volunteer information. Be
polite and noncommittal.

"Partners? In what?"

"We own a restaurant."

"I thought you are an art dealer?"

"I am."

"Peculiar, don't you think?"

"How so?"

"Restaurants and art galleries are very different things, wouldn't you say?"

"Not really, but I do make investments, and Sidney ran a very good restaurant."

"I see."

I smile knowing full well he doesn't see at all. "Anything else Sub-commissioner?"

"One more thing, if you don't mind." He pauses, turns and says something in rapid Cantonese to the younger cop lurking menacingly behind him. He turns back to me, smiles, "Did you throw Sidney Katz out his hotel suite window?"

"No, Sub-commissioner Li. I did not!"

"Didn't Mr. Katz owe you a substantial amount of money that he refused to pay?"

"I'm not sure where you're getting your information, but you are definitely on the wrong tack. If that's all Sub-commissioner, I believe I'll retire as the day has been quite exhausting and very up-setting. I'm sure you understand."

The senior cop nods, turns and fires more rapid Cantonese at his subordinate. Perhaps one of the Church boys provided the authorities with false information about me. It's the kind of thing they'd do: place obstacles in the way of me finding out the truth about Sidney.

I knew Sidney spent some time at the Bonaparte and it wouldn't surprise me that he owed them money, but enough to kill him? It didn't make sense. The Church brothers are capable of murder, but they're also too smart to pull a stunt like that in a place like Macao. Besides, killing Sidney wouldn't get them their money.

If Sidney was in trouble, why didn't he come to me? This is a problem that creates more questions than answers. And I still haven't dealt with the real reason I'm here, Kam Won-Sook. I need to think. I head to my room to try and develop a plan of action.

"Back To Black"

I sit on the edge of the bed, staring into the mirror opposite. My head is pounding. I look like shite. Interesting. The longer I stay in London, the more I tend to use British slang. It must be a sign of a weak mind, susceptible to the influences of the local patois. Perhaps that's a good thing for someone in my trade. It allows me to fit in, a chameleon of sorts. Who is Harry Raaske, or is it DCI Caul, or am I the other one, the one I was born wh? I no longer know. I am lost. I have no idea what I'm doing. Sidney is dead by suicide, murder, or misadventure of some kind. The thought of an accident doesn't even register. My head is pounding like a jackhammer on concrete.

Once again, I lapse into the self-indulgent mental rabbit hole of the self-doubt that dominates my character. I know it must be tiring for you to read this constant navel-gazing. Chalk it up to the cost of doing business with a pretend spy. Perhaps it's the source of my charm, or why else would the lovely ladies that prop up my ego ever bother with me? I should take one of my six quid headache tablets, but I decide to close my eyes instead, just for a second to block out the visual noise...

For some reason, I find myself in a closet. Harriet is pushed up close to me, thrust forward by the wardrobe of expensive men's suits and ties, the kind worn by the Church brothers. I feel Harriet's body against mine. She is purposefully closer than she needs to be. She is a tease. I love it, and she knows it. My body responds instinctively. She smiles. "Still love me, Harry?"

"Harry! Wake-up!"

I open my eyes. I'm lying on the bed with my feet hanging over the edge at the knees. Harriet is leaning over me, close, very close. She smiles. "You look exhausted, my dear. Are you alright?"

I nod, trying to shake the cobwebs from my over-taxed brain. Is this still a dream, or has Harriet's flesh-and-blood body awakened my senses? She moves off me and onto the chair at the writing desk at the side of the room. I don't bother questioning how she got in. Why bother? She often appears and disappears as if by some David Copperfield act of diversion.

"You smell good."

"Well, thank you, my love, you smell pretty nice yourself. Just like I remember."

"It's been a while."

"Yes, my love, it has, but as your English sleuths are fond of saying: "the game is afoot" and so my appearance becomes essential."

"I don't think the English actually say stuff like that unless your name is Sherlock. Besides, as you know, I am only half-British."

"Aah, a half-breed is it; that explains a lot." I give her a disapproving glare, but she knows my heart isn't in it.

"You do still love me, don't you, Harry?"

"Funny... that's what you said in my dream."

"You dream about me, Harry?" I avoid the question. She smiles, moves to the bed, and kisses me. "You know, Harry, I am very jealous of Mercury, but at least we are still partners. Aren't we Harry, partners?" She knows we are and will always be, no matter how long it has been between unscheduled rendezvouses.

"Well then, dear Watson, throw some water on your handsome face and prepare for the evening ahead. I am taking you out for a drink."

"Harriet, it's one o'clock in the morning."

"I am aware, but this is a place that Mr. Harry Raaske must visit before he leaves Macao."

We hop into a taxi that takes us from the hotel to the entertainment district. The cab stops in front of a place that looks like something out of a 1940s spy thriller starring Orson Welles. The place sits on the corner with double front folding doors facing all four points on the compass; it's a place designed for a quick getaway.

Intricate carved dark-stained wood panels form the building's sidewalls. Chinese lanterns bracket the front door. They hang down from the over-hanging balcony that wraps around the building. I almost expect Suzie Wong to step out onto the balcony in a sexy red cheongsam with a dramatic hip-high slit up the side. A miniature brass mon-key tops the front door, letting people know they've arrived at the correct place.

I stand and stare, mesmerized by the scene. The doors are open. Red-tinged light spills out onto the street, inviting us to enter if we dare. Stand-ing directly in front, we can see back to the end of the interior where there's a stage with a beau-tiful dark-haired woman in a short black cocktail dress sitting legs-crossed on a Chinese Chippendale. Behind her is an eight-foot-high, five-foot-wide version of the bar's namesake, The Brass Monkey. The woman is bracketed by a jazz quartet, dressed in black suits, white shirts, and loosened skinny black ties. They start to play the introduction to Amy Winehouse's "Back To Black". She starts to sing. She is as talented as she is beautiful. Harriet squeezes my hand. "I thought you would approve." We enter the bar. I instinctively scan the room for trouble. Harriet spots it first.

A man and woman sit at a table in a darkened recess of the bar. The woman is Kam Won-Sook. I can only see the back of the head of the man facing her. A third person joins them. It is one of the Churches. Harriet grips my hand tighter, directing me to a strategically located table in the opposite corner of the bar. Before our keisters even hit the black lacquered Chinese Chippendales, an attractive waitress delivers two drinks. She speaks with the sing-song inflection of a Cantonese accent, "A Vodka Collins for the gentleman, and a house special Brass Monkey for the lady."

"We didn't order anything."

The waitress smiles, "Compliments of the gentleman." She points to a table behind us. We turn.

A shadowy figure reaches up to a darkened sconce that hangs just within his reach. He twists the bulb ever so slightly bringing the bulb to life. A reddish-amber glow emanates from the ornate sconce highlighting his face like a Rembrandt portrait. Both Harriet and I missed him. A dangerous error. But now we know why. The face of the other Church smiles back at us. He gets up and approaches our table. He sits. He looks over at his brother, Kam, and the mysterious third man. He turns back. "Fancy meeting you here, Harry. 'Of all the gin joints in all the towns in the world, *you* walk into *this one*.' See Harry, I, too, am a bit of a movie buff. Who's your lady friend?"

Harriet leans over as if to whisper something in his ear. I see him visibly stiffen. Harriet's eyes motion me to look under the table. She is holding a six-inch blade that she has plunged into the seat cushion between his legs. "Oh, I see, she is that kind of lady friend."

"What the hell are you and Carlyle doing here with Kam?"

"Come now, Harry, you were there. She tried to kill us. In our book, that's unfinished business."

"Who's the third wheel?"

"You don't recognize your partner, Harry? How very disappointing for him."

"Sidney? He's supposed to be dead.

"*Supposed to be*, being the operative phrase."

"You faked the whole thing?"

"Just a mere sleight-of-hand, a diversion of sorts." Carlyle smiles. "Poor old Harry, how hard is it for someone like me to get a fresh body to throw out a twenty-fifth-floor window. To be honest, breaking the damn glass was the hardest part. The window was a real bitch. I'll tell you this, when that stiff hit the hotel portico from that height... well, let's just say ID became irrelevant. This is China, or at least, it might as well be. No one will bother checking too carefully. Sidney's room, Sidney's corpse."

"Just what the hell have you got him involved in?"

I notice Harriet's hand under the table move ever so slightly. He stiffens one more time. "Harry, my friend, does your Mercury know about this one?"

"She does... indeed."

"How very modern of you, old chap."

"About Sidney?"

"More unfinished business, I'm afraid... Ouch! Jesus, I think she drew blood." He catches his breath. "Not to worry, Harry, your friend owes us a favour, but in this instance, he is the doer and not the do-ee."

"Cancel it, Carson, cancel it, or there will be consequences."

"I'm afraid you are out of the loop on this one, old boy. You are deemed too close to those wild and crazy Yang brothers of the People's Republic. The mandarins in Vauxhall Cross had a change of heart. They want Kam dead. Why do you think..." he turns to look at Harriet, "...she's here?"

"I'm just back-up, my love, back-up, just in case the Church boys don't do what they were told."

"Why them? And why Sidney?"

Harriet: "It seems the Church brothers have been very bad boys. They had your friend, Sidney, bug your new restaurant/gallery thing, but it appears your partner's conscience got the best of him, so he bailed. Of course, the suits at head office were watching the whole thing. They figure Kam is still an RGB-MSS asset that your pal, Guozhi, wants placed inside MI6, so she can report back on whatever she finds of use, and just about everything is deemed of use. Eliminating Kam is essential. It is the price that needs to be paid, so the Church boys stay out of Her Majesty's Belmarsh."

I turn to Carson. "And Sidney?"

"He owes us a favour. So why get our suits bloodied? This way, everybody is happy, and all debts are paid in full."

"Well, I'm not fucking happy. I am putting a stop to this nonsense." I push back my chair to stand, but Harriet reaches out with her free hand to grab me. "Harry, stop! Let it play out. It needs to be done. Guozhi and his brother are playing us. Kam is still on the RGB-MSS payroll."

"Sidney's no hitman, Harriet."

"That's why the rest of us are here."

I remain seated. The three of us watch as Carlyle Church gets up from the table and heads for the door. As he does, Sidney removes his hand from his suit pocket. He keeps it under the table. The beautiful dark-haired singer finishes her rendition of "Back To Black."

There's an enthusiastic round of applause that drowns-out the compressed pop, pop, pop of Sidney's silenced semiautomatic. Kam slumps head-down on the table. Sidney quickly rises to push her back upright in her seat. No-one is paying attention except Harriet, Carson, and me. Sidney whispers something in Kam's ear, but even from across the room, you can see her eyes have the faraway stare of the dead. We watch as Sidney leaves.

Harriet: "We should go."

Carson: "I have a car waiting."

We get up and leave The Brass Monkey, the hangout of the original Harry Raaske. As we exit through the front doors, a black limo pulls up. The back door flings open. It's Roger, fucking, Ames. Carlyle Church is driving. Carson gets in the front seat beside his brother. I hear a scream coming from inside the bar. Someone has noticed Kam Won-Sook wouldn't be paying her tab.

Roger: "Get in!"

Epilogue
Dissimulation
...the act of hiding under a false appearance

There once was a spider who lived in a tree.
Where everything that landed would no longer be.
There once was a bee that landed on her web.
The next time we looked, the thing it was dead.
The spider was pretty and seductive to all.
And all that did land there were destined to fall.

Things are not always what they appear to be. Take the spider, for example, it can have many disguises, but all are focused on a singleminded objective: devour whatever finds its way into its web. And like the deadly Ant Mimic Jumping Spider or the less than appetizing Bird Dung Spider, the spy also hides in plain sight, ready to strike those that dare enter their web. But, it is possible for a spider to get caught in her own complex trap, perhaps by mistake, perhaps by carelessness, or perhaps by sheer arrogance. The notion of being *hoisted on one's own petard* is especially true in the business of intelligence, where intelligence is often sorely lacking. An overly elaborate gambit is like a meal with so many coatings of sauce, the source of the meat becomes completely unrecognizable.

The game may be afoot as Harriet so artfully quipped, but need to know compartmentalization and mixed contrary agendas have led to an overly convoluted playing field with so many layers of diversion and deceit, the players may just have forgotten exactly who the enemy is. I am not happy. In truth, I am pissed, and both Harriet and Roger know it.

Roger: "You look a bit distressed, old boy."

Harriet: "Don't be angry, darling. The plan has worked, and the players are in place."

"Well, isn't that just fucking lovely?" I turn to Roger. "You read-in these two thugs but not me. You involve my friend, an amateur, and hang me out to dry. What the hell is going on?"

"Circumstances, dear boy, your friend, Sidney and the Church boys were all in need of a get-out-of-prison card, and each of them just happened to be in a position to earn one. Word came down from on-high that Kam Won-Sook had to go, so the Church brothers were given the assignment. Your pal Sidney was already in Macao, so he was brought in to help. Since dead men can't be assassins, the fake suicide was arranged. The authorities would assume Sidney was dead, so how could he be the killer?"

"Jesus, Roger, that's nuts!"

"Maybe, but it worked. Embedding Kam in England was Guozhi's brother's idea as a favour to his friends in Pyongyang, but Guozhi didn't trust the North Koreans, his brother, or Kam. He must have figured the British would find out and eliminate her, damaging the already delicate RGB-MSS relationship. He knew Sidney owed everybody money, including you, and that the Churches wanted Kam dead, so Guozhi authorized them to recruit Sidney to kill her, not knowing we had already arranged the same thing. But once Sidney was brought in, Guozhi's scheme got more complicated. He wants Sidney to reimplement the Churches' failed eavesdropping plan, but this time, Quandary is the target."

"You know, Roger, spiders can get caught in their own webs if they're not careful, and Sidney is an amateur at this game."

"True, old boy, true, but in your metaphor is the careless spider Sidney or Guozhi? Remember, it wasn't that long ago that you were an amateur spider. In any case, Guozhi paid Sydney's debt and got the Churches to set it all up. The Church brothers may be bad boys, but they're not traitors. They informed Vauxhall Cross, and the brass decided to let it play-out. Kam would be eliminated and Sidney would be positioned to feed Guozhi misinformation. It's the perfect double-cross."

"Jesus, Roger, when plans get this convoluted, things are bound to go sideways. Besides, how are you going to explain Sidney being alive?"

"Already done, dear boy. Hotel records show that Sidney exchanged rooms with another guest who had just lost substantial sums of money at the casino and was despondent. His only option was suicide. The paperwork on the room change hadn't been processed by the hotel staff when the police originally investigated. Mr. Li was quite cooperative in making it all happen."

"I'm sure he was. How much did that cost us?"

"Mr. Li was well-compensated for his efforts. And I very much doubt he would want the authorities to find out what really happened."

"So what happens in Macao, stays in Macao?"

"Exactly, dear boy, Macao police aren't going to follow-up on some British stiff. Guozhi thinks his plan is working. And we can feed him any misleading information we think will help us. A job well done, old son."

"We'll see Roger. We'll see." I look out the window of the limo and notice we are not returning to the hotel. "Where are we going now?"

Harriet takes my hand. "To the airport, my love. Your hotel bill has been paid, your suitcase is in the boot, and the charter is waiting."

Back at The Brass Monkey, the singer has left the stage and made her way back to the kitchen. She spots a dish of tiger shrimp forgotten in the mayhem caused by the discovery of the now-deceased Kam Won-Sook. The beautiful dark-haired *chanteuse* picks up one of the shrimp and places it in her mouth. She feels the presence of someone close.

Haru Endo, steps out from between the kitchen counters, "Is it done?"

The singer swallows the remnants of the shrimp. "Yes. It's done."

"Call the Minister."

She takes her mobile phone from the small black leather purse that hangs from her naked shoulder. "Yang *Guoanbu*, t*he Katz' in the cradle"*.

Minister of State Yang Guozhi, hangs up his telephone. He looks down at the open three files in front of him, each one with a photograph and a dossier: one for Harry Raaske, one for Sydney Katz, and one for Haru Endo.

THE END

Deception

The world is a dangerous place, and every country has men and women tasked to protect it. These people go by many names: secret agent, intelligence officer, and analyst are just a few. Harry is one such person. He is an analyst. He spends his time reading, researching, and analyzing, followed by writing reports that often never see the light of day.

Harry is well educated with a seemingly important job, but Harry is bored. Bored, because analysts never get to be the hero, never get to order cocktails stirred not shaken, and, never, never, get the girl. Harry is frustrated, frustrated because his superiors told him the report he just spent six months working on is to be tabled, and no, he can't have a field operative to work with to follow up.

Harry has one very dangerous character flaw, he has an imagination, not something the men on the Top Floor appreciate. Harry needs to prove himself; he needs some excitement in his life, and that excitement comes in a deadly package of intrigue and murder that combines something called the *Sister Project* with a Russian master spy, H, K. Kyrsa, code name, the *Beautiful Rat*, and the devastatingly gorgeous Harriet. The question is, is it all just happening in Harry's head, or is there a real plot that needs to be stopped? Is Harry just plain crazy, or are the Russians out to mess with the West one more time? Harry is on his own, not sure who to trust. Are there any good guys in the world of espionage? The only way to find out is to find Kyrsa, the Beautiful Rat. Join Harry in his search for what may not even be real.

Delusion: Lucy's Breath

On a chilly November New York City morning in 1953, a scientist working for the CIA on psychotropic mind-control experiments walked off the tenth-floor balcony of the Statler Hotel. He had become increasingly disenchanted with the bizarre and incredibly dangerous work he had been doing in service to national security. Despite the patriotic rationale, the scientist felt his life's work was immoral and most certainly illegal. He wanted out, unfortunately, he knew too much, and knowing too much is a very precarious position to be in if you work for a clandestine operation run by America's very own version of Josef Mengele, the Angel of Death.

The scientist insisted on getting out, and out he got, through the window and off the balcony of the Statler Hotel on that brisk Fall morning in Manhattan. Was suicide his solution for terminating his deal with the devil or did the devil do him in? It's impossible to say. The evidence although in plain sight is murky and blurred by time and the self-preservation of those responsible. I know what you're thinking, not in my America, not in my beloved United States, not in the home of the brave and the land of the free. Unfortunately, it did happen; it's the kind of thing that happens when governments feel an existential threat.

America has a fundamental flaw, an Achilles heel of perspective and attitude; it fails to understand history and its place in it. In the words of philosopher, George Santayana, "Those who cannot remember the past are condemned to repeat it." If you believe it can't happen here, I urge you to take a look at The Wall Street Putsch of 1933, and the name of one of the participants. You might find it informative. It could happen again. America is under siege by a series of existential threats. It's not some crackpot conspiracy theory; it's history. The question I have is: which is more dangerous, the external threat or the internal threat?

For those who cling to Senator Barry Goldwater's Cold War aphorism, "Extremism in defence of liberty is no vice." I urge you to remember the past because if you don't, you will be condemned to a future you did not expect and an existence you will be forced to endure.

What follows could happen, and maybe will happen if you allow extremism to take hold of the levers of power.

Dilemma: Mozart's Medicine

A poisoned accountant, a Chinese painter with an infamous Italian name, the People's Minister of Science
and Technology, his brother the Director of the Enterprise Division of the Ministry of State Security, and
Harry, the art dealer who moonlights as a Secret Intelligence Service agent are the players in the search
for why D. D. Greyson was poisoned by a seventeenth-
century Italian cosmetic favoured by disillusioned
wives.

The business of intelligence is often referred to as
information gathering. A simple proposition: gather
enough data so the politicians can make informed,
rational decisions on things like national security, or
on whether or not one of the several competing
forces in the world is about to go all ballistic on your
ass. But the problem is not too little information, but
too much. There are cameras everywhere and facial
recognition software that allows agencies to track
anyone's movement day and night. The various intelligence services have so much information at their
disposal, it becomes difficult to decide what is relevant, actionable, or even real. It is the paradox of
choice, paralysis of analysis, or if you prefer, the spy's
dilemma. No one knows what is real, what is noise, or
what is purposeful misdirection.

And so our hero, Harry, becomes a player, not because
he is particularly brave or expert in the art of manip-
ulation or even killing, but rather because he has an
imagination. He is a man who can conjure reality out
of abstraction and that particular skill can be a very
important asset when it comes to playing three-play-
er Chinese checkers with competing Beijing interests.

The worlds of art and national security collide on the streets of London leaving a trail of burned paintings, payoffs, dead bodies, and deadly microchips.

The Outlaw Rider
"If you're not prepared to cheat,
you're not prepared to win."

Jesse James, the daughter of a deceased mob-connected rug salesman, becomes a jockey working for the *Hong Mian* triad in order to feed winners to State Senator Samuel Somersby. The Senator is responsible for approving California gaming licenses. To date, only Native CANGV casinos are allowed to have slots. California horse racing will die if they aren't allowed to add slot machines to their venues. Benson Yeung, Dragon Head of the *Hong Mian* triad, and his chief lieutenant, Johnny Luck, have a plan to force Somersby to approve their Native partner's demands for off-reservation gaming licenses. At the center of the plan is a unique white thoroughbred Spirit horse, prized by Native people, appropriately named Medicine Hat.

Dead End
There Are No Good Guys

It all started five years earlier with the murder of Peter Pretty Boy Chen, a low-level soldier for Benson Yeung's Hong Mian triad. Rumor had it that the Guan Yu statue that sat on the old man's desk, the symbol of his Dragon Head status as leader of the Hong Mian, was filled with priceless Pigeon Blood rubies, or at least that's what Peter Pretty Boy Chen thought. Whether he was right or wrong is a tale for another time and another place.

What's significant is, his desire to get his hands on those rubies led to his brains being splattered all over the wall of the Green Dragon Restaurant. Like all classic California mysteries the past is never forgotten or forgiven; it always comes back to raise its ugly head.

Fast forward five years. We first met Jesse James and her associates in *The Outlaw Rider*, when she was a young female jockey making a name for herself on the track and off under the guidance of her mentor, triad big shot, Johnny Luck. Jesse has moved up the Hong Mian ladder and has made herself a major triad player, but the past is never so far behind that it doesn't affect the present. And so *Dead End* begins.

Palermo
A Place To Die

The race took place in picturesque Palermo, Sicily, but this wasn't your typical horse race with rules designed to protect the horses, jockeys, and bettors; this was a Mafia sponsored street race: a blood sport free-for-all more suited for the Coliseum than the back-streets of the scenic Sicilian town. Race promoter, Santos Luzzato, nephew to Nicky The Mushroom Fungo, wanted in on his American Uncle's horse racing connections with the LA triads. The race leads to a series of decisions that end with a suspicious car accident that kills billionaire heiress and racehorse owner, Josephine Somersby Murphy, sister to the Governor of California, Samuel Somersby, a man with Presidential ambitions and ties to Johnny Luck, LA triad big shot.

Love, sex, murder, and racehorses create a toxic mix of intrigue and suspense that drives Luck's protégé, Jesse James, to Sicily, Argentina, England, and Switzerland in her pursuit of the truth. Who killed Josephine Murphy? Was it Luzzato, Nicky Fungo, Murphy's brother, the Governor, or was it someone closer to Jesse. Palermo, a place to die.

Stone Cold
Between a Stone and a Hard Place

On the surface, Major William Stone (Retired) is merely a rich, English expatriate with a diverse military and financial services background now living in Palermo, Argentina where he runs a small art gallery along with his assistant Margarita Cervantes.

If you scratch the surface, you'll find that Stone was recently the chauffeur for Mrs. Josephine Murphy, heiress to the Murphy Peanut Butter Company, the largest peanut butter manufacturer in the USA, and owner of numerous expensive thoroughbred racehorses. This seemingly incongruous set of circumstances gets even more intriguing when you learn that Stone inherited over one billion dollars when Josephine Murphy died in a tragic, and somewhat questionable, car accident in the hills of Palermo, Sicily leaving Major Stone the bulk of her estate.

After the Murphy estate is settled, Stone disappears to reemerge in Argentina leading a quiet and peaceful life as a wealthy art gallery owner and financier. His good fortune is tempered by the fact he left the love of his life, Jesse James, protégé to gangster Johnny Luck, back in LA.

The problem is, Major William Stone died in the Falkland Islands and the man now assuming his modified identity is disgraced MI6 financial wizard Jacob Conrad. Conrad took the fall for his Vauxhall Cross masters' illegal shenanigans ending up in jail with a lengthy prison term. According to the British newspaper reports, Conrad died in Belmarsh Prison, only to be resurrected by Section Six's cyber boffins as William Stone, international financial consultant living in Hong Kong, where he runs into Charlie Long,

Dragon Head of the Wan Chai and a major rival of the Hong Mian, led by Benson Yeung and Johnny Luck.

Stone Cold dives deep into the back-story of how Jacob Conrad becomes William Stone, why he disappeared leaving Jesse behind, and who'll control the flow of cocaine into the USA. From Hong Kong to Palermo, London, Cacaloxuchitl, Mexico and Los Angeles, this is a tale of secret agents, drug dealers, money launders, and murders, all wrapped in a delicious recipe of greed, envy, cocaine, and peanut butter chilli.

The Aussie Switch
Published By MRPwebmedia

Horse trainers, Davey and Pauly Cisco are looking for a fresh start in Southern California after wearing out their welcome in their native Australia. The Cisco twins are identical in looks but not personality; Pauly, like most horse trainers, pushes the envelope of acceptable practice, while his look-alike brother rips through regulations with regularity and abandon. It didn't take long for the two brothers to hook-up with a couple of conmen: an expert computer hacker who likes e-gaming and a shyster stock promoter on the lookout for eager marks willing to blow their fortunes on a shady horse-betting consortium. The one thing they didn't count on is an associate of Benson Yeung's Hong Mian triad; an ex-South Korean Colonel who operates a crooked international gambling empire. Two corrupt confidence men, unethical twin horse trainers, and doppelgänger thoroughbreds add up to a combustible confluence of confusion, miss-direction, and murder, with tentacles that twist their way through LA, Sidney, Hong Kong, Seoul, and Macao.

Ballet of Bullets
The Game Is Dodging Death
Published By MRPwebmedia

Internet gambling and the expansion of casinos beyond the Nevada State Line have put a financial strain on racetracks. Johnny Luck, Hong Mian triad big shot, and his beautiful blonde ex-jockey protege, Jesse James, are always on the lookout for ways to expand the triad's gambling operation. Back in the fifties and sixties, Jai Alai was a big deal in Florida. Gamblers would fill the *frontons* and drop thousands of dollars betting on Basque athletics competing in a sport that was so dangerous it was referred to as the Ballet of Bullets and The Game Is Dodging Death.

Johnny Luck sees the potential revenue that could be produced by resurrecting the all but dead blood sport. The question is, how to make it popular again? Jesse has the answer. Television. People will bet on anything; they will also watch anything, as witnessed by the plethora of cooking shows that feature ordinary people competing for who can fry the best egg.

If there's a competition, people will bet on who will win. But where there is money, there is corruption; enter the Miami Bettor's Club, run by old Hong Mian rivals Tommy The King Kong and Marco Antonia Suarez, nicknamed *El Astronauta*. In the end, the Ballet of Bullets becomes all too real for the people fighting for control of the gambling revenue generated by the International Jai Alai League.

What's Your Poison?
How Cocktail's Got Their Names
Published By MRPwebmedia

Why do we call mixed alcohol drinks "cocktails"? How do they get their exotic names: names like the Singapore Sling, Screw Driver, the Alamagoozlum, the Angel's Kiss, the Hanky Panky, the Harvey Wallbanger, Sex On The Beach, the Monkey Gland, the Brass Monkey, the Margarita, the Japalac, the Lion's Tail, and many, many more? Who makes up these names, where are they invented, why, and how do you make them? These questions will be answered in *"What's Your Poison?"* by exploring the incidents, people, and places that prompted the creation of these exotic concoctions.

Cowboys, Lawmen, & Outlaws

When we think of the Old West, it seems like ancient history, but historically it was yesterday. Many of the characters of the post Civil War Old West lived well into the twentieth century: Bat Masterson died in 1921 and Wyatt Earp didn't pass-on until 1929. Josie Bassett, one of the Wild Bunch girls managed to hang on until 1963 and she only died then because she got kicked in the head by a horse.

History doesn't end with an era, remnants, artifacts, and people overlap. History doesn't stop because technology and style move on.

The future is more likely to look like the film *Brazil* with its jury-rigged conglomeration of antique flotsam and modern-day technological jetsam, than the bright shiny newness of *Star Trek*. Turning history into fantasy is dangerous; it leads to mistaken notions and bad decisions. Maybe it's time to grow up and see the heroes of the Old West, as they really were, cowboys, lawmen, and outlaws.

Organized Crime Queens
The Secret World of Female Gangsters

From the bizarre world of female Japanese motorcycle gangs to the historic rise and fall of London's Forty Elephants, the history of female organized crime is both fascinating and strange. These are the stories, both true and legendary of the female crime bosses that broke the mould of feminine gentility. This is The Secret World of Female Gangsters.

www.ingramcontent.com/pod-product-compliance
Lightning Source LLC
Chambersburg PA
CBHW051252170626
46809CB00004B/1619